0

————————————— ★ —————————————

At that moment the phone rang. We were both startled but the colour drained from Vanessa's face as though her blood pressure had just dropped thirty points.

"I'll get it," I said as I lifted my arm to pick up the receiver.

Vanessa's hand cracked down on mine. "Leave it," she said. "Let it ring."

"But…" I began to protest.

"It's him," she said. "He knows we're here."

It took a few seconds for her words to register. *He knows we're here. We. We!*

There was no doubt about it. He was after me, too.

————————————— ★ —————————————

"…intriguing and unusual, with the flavor of a classic English novel."
—*The Midwest Book Review*

"A clever and intriguing mystery."
—*Rendezvous*

CHRISTINE GREEN
DEADLY ADMIRER

WORLDWIDE.

TORONTO • NEW YORK • LONDON
AMSTERDAM • PARIS • SYDNEY • HAMBURG
STOCKHOLM • ATHENS • TOKYO • MILAN
MADRID • WARSAW • BUDAPEST • AUCKLAND

DEADLY ADMIRER

A Worldwide Mystery/December 1996

This edition is reprinted by arrangement with Walker and Company.

ISBN 0-373-26223-X

Printed in U.S.A.

For Richard and the girls, V.J. and K.C.
With all my love.

ONE

ON SATURDAY NIGHTS the inhabitants of Longborough are either indoors watching television or out eating, drinking, fornicating or fighting. The casualty department of Longborough General sees the results.

This Saturday was busier than most. At two a.m. we were still full, each bay containing the result of a misspent Saturday evening. All still alive, bar one. He, poor chap, had died as a result of irregularity. Irregular drinking and even more irregular sex.

He and his common-law wife had been out celebrating his retirement from his job as a postman. He'd drunk at least six whiskies and the light of love had shone once again. Its candle had flared only briefly and then been snuffed out. He had died post-coitally, another Saturday night victim.

His wife seemed more peeved than distressed.

'Just like him,' she said, as she unbuttoned her grey coat, her face flushed with the oppressive hospital warmth. Later, she would be pale and trembly when the realisation came that no amount of nagging would ever stir him into action again. For the moment, however, annoyance buoyed her up, a shield against shock and misery.

'Just like him,' she repeated. 'He always rolled over and went to sleep afterwards. This time though, he didn't wake up. Selfish pig!'

She accepted my offer of tea and I sat her down in the room, no bigger than a cupboard, that we reserve for grieving relatives.

My companion nurse, Jane Simons, continued to cope with the observations of the more serious patients while I went to put the kettle on.

The ward 'kitchen' contained three wooden chairs, an electric cooker with only two rings working and a fridge. On one of the chairs sat the casualty officer, Ben Haselbech. He was fast asleep, with his straight fair hair flopping over his forehead. It seemed a crime to wake him but with just the three of us on duty it was impossible to cope without him. I made the tea and placed a mug on the table and then, kneeling down, I shook him gently by the shoulder.

'Oh, God!' he said after several shakes. 'I dreamt I was in my bed. It was wonderful. What's going on?'

'Nothing's changed. We're still full. The registrars haven't turned up yet and I've checked the bed statement. We've only three empties.'

'Bloody typical,' he said as he swept his hair back from his forehead. 'Is that tea for me?' he asked, glancing at the full mug.

I nodded. 'Will you have a word with Mrs Flore? She's in the relatives' room.'

'Can't you do it, Kate?'

I shook my head. 'You'll have to tell her about the postmortem. I'll speak to her afterwards.'

'Okay,' he said reluctantly, 'I'm on my way.'

The night wore on. Mrs Flore sadly left her late husband behind and we carried on working solidly. By four a.m. we had patched up, discharged, reassured and performed a minor miracle—casualty was empty.

All three of us had just sat down exhausted in reception when a young woman walked in. She was wearing a black tracksuit and white trainers and surveyed us over the top of the counter.

'Please, I need help.' She spoke calmly. 'I've just taken an overdose.'

We weren't surprised at what she'd done. Saturday night was ever popular as a time that proved life's disappointments. Sometimes, though, I thought Saturday night was *the* night, only because Sunday followed and to the lonely and afraid Sunday offers only *Songs of Praise* on TV and the promise of work on Monday. What did surprise us was her calmness and the fact that she came in alone. Most people bring a friend, or a relative or both.

Scrabbling to our feet, the three of us stood up as guiltily as if we'd been caught by the general manager pilfering aspirin. Ben guided her to a chair and began to fill out the medical notes.

Once we'd had an all-night receptionist but cut-backs meant that from midnight we were on our own. Even the porter deserted us to collect bodies from the ward or do security patrols of the ward areas.

'Paracetamol and sleeping pills—Temazepam—they are prescribed,' she said in a low-pitched, rather gentle voice.

Ben didn't usually have much patience with would-be suicides but for her he managed a kind smile.

'How many have you taken?' he asked.

'Fifteen,' she replied, 'of each.'

'When?'

'Just now,' she said. 'A few minutes ago. I drove here straight away.'

'Staff Nurse,' he said, giving me a friendly wink, 'do your bit—stat!'

Doing my bit meant giving the stomach a wash out and stat meant pronto.

Paracetamol kills. Not instantly, as many desperate to die think, but slowly, cruelly, poisoning the liver, making you vomit, making your head bang, making your last days or weeks worse than anything you ever suffered before.

Vanessa Wootten was thirty-one but looked twenty-five. She had the sort of elfin face that lasts well, a clear pale skin and large blue eyes full of unshed tears and misery. A fresh bruise had marked her cheekbone but even that didn't diminish her beauty. Her blonde hair, cut short, was jauntily spiky on top, and from her delicate ears golden circles hung. I wondered when she had felt happy or hopeful enough to put on those earrings.

I walked with her to one of the six empty bays, pulled the green-leaved curtains around the nearest bay and helped her clamber on to the trolley. Then I began my explanation of the inglorious technique of stomach wash out.

'There's no need to explain,' she said with a wry smile, 'I'm a district nurse. If you give me the tube I'll swallow it myself.'

The wash out trolley stood in permanent readiness in one of the treatment rooms and I trundled it in and lubricated the tube to make the passage down her gullet easier. Laying the tube on ice makes the tube stiffer and even easier, but there was no ice in readiness and no time to waste.

'Pretend it's a piece of steak,' I suggested, which was my usual patter and works well, although since I've been saying it I can't seem to cope with steak any more.

Bravely she took the tube and began to swallow. I found myself gulping with her, willing the tube to go down easily and sighing when finally it was down her oesophagus and into her stomach. She then positioned herself on her side and I began to syphon warm water via the stomach tube in, and out again, in and out again, until after a while my arm began to ache. Finally I once more raised the funnel and drained out the last of the deadly solution into the bucket.

As I worked I murmured nursely encouragements: 'Soon be over,' and 'Just relax, breathe easily,' and 'Not long now.' Sayings that did more to reassure me than perhaps my patient.

Eventually the water ran clear and I slowly eased up the tube and used a tissue to wipe the moisture gently from nose and mouth.

I left her for a while to rest. Dr Haselbech had found the strength to get to his bed and Jane was tidying up the minor ops theatre. Vanessa Wootten's first ordeal was at an end.

'Found out why she did it, Kate?' Jane asked as she placed a fresh white paper sheet on the theatre table.

'I haven't asked her yet. I wanted to give her time to recover first.'

'No doubt some man's given her the elbow. Is she very disturbed?'

'She's as cool as yesterday's rhubarb. Not even a tear yet.'

'Well, that's good,' said Jane, 'because Ben wants you to try to assess her mental condition and keep her here for a few hours until he's had a sleep. Then he'll refer her to the psychiatric registrar, if necessary.'

'And what if she doesn't want to stay?'

Jane shrugged. 'You're the qualified psychiatric nurse.'

She left me to continue with the tidying, her tall slim body swaying as she walked, as fragile-looking as a newly planted sapling. Appearances were deceptive: Jane, although young, was stalwart oak, with an appetite like a navvy and, when she chose, language that could match any drunken football hooligan. The casualty porter at the first hint of trouble would cower behind her, while she stood imperiously before the most obnoxious trouble-maker giving them verbal hell.

Vanessa lay on the trolley, eyes closed, hands folded defensively across her chest. I stood and watched her for a while, wondering if she had felt as I had on my thirtieth birthday. I'd woken mildly miserable that morning, received five cards, one from Hubert, and had spent most of the day reading a book called *Your Aging Process*. From it I gleaned that I would get shorter in height, my brain cells would disappear and indeed had been disappearing for years, and my nose would continue to grow for ever. Information so depressing should be banned. For weeks afterwards I became obsessed with measuring my nose. It was still quite small and didn't seem to be growing at any calculable rate so I stopped worrying. What did it matter anyway? Would I really mind being four foot ten, thin-boned, shapeless and with a long nose when I was eighty? I decided that with my eyesight on the wane and my brain cells in single figures I'd probably be quite satisfied with myself.

At the moment I was five foot four, a size fourteen, had good skin, and eyes that were greenish-blue on bad days and turquoise on good days. I had no deformities, few friends, but no known enemies either. I'd resolved then that no other birthday would upset me quite so much again.

'I expect you wonder why I did it?' Vanessa's voice shook me from my self-indulgent reverie.

I nodded.

She smiled at me and said quietly, 'I expect you think my boyfriend's ditched me.'

'Could be a reason,' I agreed.

'Well it wasn't that. I ditched him. I'd been trying to ditch him for ages. Every time he threatened suicide. Once he slashed his wrists, another time he drove the car into a tree. Wrecked the tree, he came out without a scratch. He made my life a living hell. Tantrums, emotional blackmail. So this time, though, I thought I'd show him I really meant it. He'd have to accept the breakup then, wouldn't he? It was only a gesture really, but once I'd started I couldn't stop. He left after seeing me take the first few. I realised then that he'd wanted me to die. He'd probably wanted it all along. Then no one else could have me. I seem to attract nutters. By the time I'd swallowed the lot I realised he'd be getting just what he wanted. So I came here.'

'How do you feel now?' Which was a daft question but she smiled.

'I feel exhausted, but relaxed, sort of dreamy.'

I supposed that was how a bucket of water away from death might make me feel too.

'Do you want to talk any more or shall I let you rest?' I asked, trying to be diplomatic.

'I do have another problem,' she said. 'I'm sorry to be a nuisance.'

I could believe that. I'd found during the time I'd worked in casualty that most overdose victims struggled with far more than just one problem. 'Try me. I'm a good listener. And sometimes it helps to talk. Puts a new perspective on things.'

She stared at me for a moment. 'Are you married?'

I shook my head. 'I'm thirty,' I answered, as if that was a bench-mark for spinsterhood. 'I lived with some-one once. He died, an accident. Since then I suppose I've been ultra-fussy or ultra-wary. Anyway, the men I meet seem to think I'm either tempestuous or forever randy. Their disappointment is agonising to watch.'

Vanessa didn't smile, she frowned. 'I'm being fol-lowed,' she whispered. 'A man is following me. Some-times during the day, sometimes in the evening. He's watching me. I think he wants to kill me.'

Uncharitably the first word that came to mind was paranoia, but I couldn't remember much about it except that people imagine they are being persecuted.

Before I could comment, Vanessa said, 'I know you don't believe me. I've been to the police. They don't be-lieve me. They think I'm a neurotic woman who is prob-ably lonely. I might be lonely but I'm not imagining being followed; he...'

She tailed off as if having told me she had said too much. I had to make a quick decision—was she mad or not? I decided, intuitively, that she was sane, but very frightened. And although I suspected that her boyfriend was probably the man in question, she still needed help. He sounded much more loopy than she did.

'I may be able to help you,' I said. 'My name's Kate Kinsella and I run a detective agency from an office in the High Street—above Humberstones the funeral direc-tors. Come and see me when you feel better and perhaps together we can sort this out.'

I'd made a sneaky move here and I hoped she didn't think I always found my clients this way, but her face brightened in surprise.

'How do you manage to do two jobs?'

I shrugged, trying to look modest. I didn't want her to assume that I was some sort of super-efficient jack of all trades. 'I only do occasional work here through the Berkerly Nursing Agency,' I explained. 'Just the odd night but it helps to pay for a few luxuries.'

I tried to make it sound as if my working nights were merely an optional extra. In reality I would have starved without the income.

'And do you really think you can find this man?'

'I'll have a damn good try,' I replied. 'I might be able to warn him off at least.'

'I hope you're right, Kate,' she murmured. 'I'd like to go home now.'

'The doctor wants to see you again. He'd prefer you to stay.'

'Can I discharge myself?'

'Well, you can,' I said, 'though I think you should wait to see the doctor. But if you are sure you want to go now I'll explain it to him.' I didn't say that I probably wouldn't be able to wake him. He'd been without sleep for thirty-six hours. 'It's hospital policy that all non-accidental overdoses are given a psychiatric appointment. Will you be willing to attend out-patients in a day or two?'

'Of course I'll come.'

'You'll ring tomorrow?'

She nodded. 'I'll do that. I promise. And I'll come to your office.'

She smiled then a little sadly and whispered thank you; I knew that with such a pleasant smile and such a pretty face few people would refuse her anything. In fact she still seemed as calm as she had appeared when she first arrived, but was she still a suicide risk? Pure intuition told me she wasn't. But then sometimes my intuition lets me down.

'Have you a friend who could give you a lift home and stay with you?' I asked.

Easing herself from her relaxed sideways position on the trolley Vanessa sat up properly. 'I've got my car,' she said, 'I'll be fine on my own. I do have to get to work to-morrow. That will take my mind off things. I feel fine now, really I do. You being willing to help has done that. And believing me about the man. Would you just watch me leave, though, just to... well, just to make sure?'

'Of course,' I said.

I followed her outside to the dimly lit parking bay and waited while she got into a red Mini and drove away. I waved her goodbye and then stayed for a while to make sure no one followed her. No one did. But the thought crossed my mind that out there in the darkness someone might have been waiting for her. And I'd allowed her to go.

TWO

TUESDAY IS market day in Longborough. From my office window I can see the striped tops of the stalls and the stall-holders unpacking their wares, and in good weather when I have the window open I can hear their sales patter.

This Tuesday the wind blew viciously and from behind closed windows I watched the few customers who braved the early March winds. I'd been about to abandon staring when a red Mini drew up outside Humberstones. I recognised Vanessa Wootten immediately. She was in district nurse's uniform: a navy blue coat unflatteringly long and a round pill-box hat which, as she left her car, she had to pin down with one hand. She wore flat black pumps with matching black stockings. Hubert would definitely notice.

I waited for the sound of footsteps on the stairs and as I did so opened a file so that I'd look busy.

But it was Hubert who appeared first. 'There's a Miss Vanessa Wootten to see you,' he said. 'Are you busy?'

'Frantic,' I answered. 'I'm doing a major investigation of the market. Very time-consuming. I don't think I'll be able to fit her in.'

Hubert's brown eyes glinted like oily prunes and I could see he wasn't in the mood for sarcasm so I said, 'Send her up, Hubert, will you, before she takes fright at being left at the bottom of the stairs.'

The side entrance of Humberstones, reserved for a steady flow of corpses, was only coffin wide and led into a small hall painted in dull green. From there rose two steep flights of stairs, uncarpeted and unused, apart from Hubert, me, and the very occasional client. A single purple shade covered the ceiling light and sometimes the fringe of the shade trembled with or without wind, breeze or draught. In fanciful moments I suspected the fringe only moved when a fresh corpse entered the building. A sort of salutary greeting.

Living newcomers to my part of the building were sometimes asked to wait just under the stairwell. Hubert had placed there my old jumble sale armchair, maroon floral with a sagging bottom, for clients who had serious intentions. Waiting there for a few minutes was as good as a down payment. It showed real commitment, perhaps even desperation.

Vanessa walked steadily up the stairs, her footsteps sounding loud and purposeful.

'This is an unusual place to have an office,' she said, smiling. The bruise on her face had almost faded. Now that I could see her more closely I could see just how well the blue of her uniform suited her. Even the pill-box hat managed to look cute rather than old-fashioned.

'I like it,' I said. 'It's very convenient and there aren't too many distractions, apart from watching the market in action.'

She smiled again as she sat down in one of my dove grey, courtesy of Hubert, office chairs.

'He's still following me,' she said, taking off her hat and raking her hair through with one hand.

'How are you feeling now?' I asked. 'Are you sure you feel up to answering questions?'

'I'm okay,' she said with a shrug. 'My boyfriend, Sean, came back for his belongings today and now he's gone off into the great blue yonder and all I want to do is get this other matter cleared up.'

I nodded. 'Tell me about it. From the beginning.'

She frowned and stayed silent for a while, as though she really didn't want to tell her story, for by the telling and by someone believing it, the situation might become somehow more dangerously real.

Eventually she began, and as she talked she rubbed the inside of her fingers, occasionally cracking one as she bent and straightened each slim digit in turn. 'It was about three weeks ago I first saw the car, an old black Ford Escort. I'd look in the mirror and see it... At first I didn't take much notice, especially in the early morning when traffic is heavy anyway. But then I began to notice it in the afternoon and sometimes when I went out in the evening I saw the same car parked up the road...'

'Did you take the number?'

'Of course, Kate. When I realised I wasn't imagining things, I took the number and told the police. The car had been stolen. He must have known we were on to it, because he stopped following me for a couple of days and when he started again he was driving a different car.'

'What colour is it this time?' I asked, trying to keep the increasing scepticism from my voice.

She looked hurt and didn't answer my question.

I felt guilty. 'I'm sorry, Vanessa. I didn't mean it to sound like that. Could you describe the driver to me?'

She paused for a moment and stared at some point on the wall facing her. 'I can't,' she answered miserably. 'Not properly. He always keeps well behind me. I think he's got dark hair but whenever I've tried to have a good look at him I've nearly had an accident or he's lowered his head so that I can't see his face. And I feel too scared to get a closer look.'

'How tall do you think he is?' I asked, feeling dispir-
ited about a man with no face and an ever-changing car.

'Average, I suppose. Unless he's got a cushion under
the seat.'

'Build?'

She frowned. 'Average again, I suppose. This isn't being much help, is it?'

'Not a lot,' I agreed. But I was writing everything
down and trying to decide if this case was going to be
worth while, financially or professionally.

'Can you afford to hire me?' I asked. 'I'm sure the
police will do something if this carries on.'

'I can afford it, I've got savings,' she said firmly. 'Will
two hundred a week be enough to retain you? I'll pay you
another three hundred when you catch him.'

Retain me! I thought. Two hundred a week. That was
almost enough to make me start thinking about buying
smart suits and having holidays abroad. I could buy a
new lamp for my office or a telephone answering machine or even make a down payment on a computer...

'Will you take the case then?' Vanessa was saying. 'I'll
pay you two weeks in advance.'

I tried not to appear too keen. I knew now that if she
was neurotic, at least she was a solvent neurotic and more
than willing to pay for a cure. Paying the bills had been
a problem since I opened eight months ago and Vanessa
Wootten was only the second to offer cash in advance.

'Of course,' I said, 'I'd be pleased to.'

The bank would also be pleased and so, too, would
Hubert who was always finding me the strangest people
to act for and then was disgruntled when I turned them
down.

As Vanessa left I promised to spend as much time as I could following her and hopefully following her unknown admirer.

'I hope that's what he is,' she said with a wry smile, 'an admirer.'

'What do *you* think he is?' I asked.

'I think he's a killer,' she said, fear glinting in her needle-sharp eyes.

I walked with her to the second set of stairs and watched her descend to the hallway and then pause as she gazed up at the purple fringe of the shade, watching as it fluttered very slightly. And then she turned her head upwards to look at me. Her face seemed pale in the purple gloom but it was her expression which disturbed me, and the hunted look in her eyes. But resignation was there also, as though she had seen death and it wasn't death itself that scared her, but its prelude.

Hubert came up immediately. I'd left my office door open because I knew he'd appear as soon as he saw Vanessa leave. Just lately he seemed far more interested in my prospective clients than his already dead ones.

'Is it a goer?' he asked, peering round the door.

'It's a goer,' I answered. 'And you can come in.'

He walked in and sat down on the edge of my desk, a habit which irritates me but I say nothing, thinking charitably that maybe he's trying to save the wear and tear on my office chairs.

'This one could be quite lucrative, but there are complications.'

'There usually are with you.'

'Your confidence in me, Hubert,' I said, 'is truly underwhelming.'

He smiled then, which improved his face not one jot, because his eyes seemed to disappear, leaving only shining false teeth and a nose set in a pastry-coloured skin beneath a balding head. A top hat and a sombre expression made him look relatively normal. Not that I gave him much to smile about, but he was at the moment my best friend, managing to be miserable with fortitude and occasionally enjoying a wary kind of happiness. He didn't expect much of life; knowing only too well how it all ends.

'What does she want you to do, Kate?' he asked.

'She wants me to find the man who's following her.'

Hubert's eyes rolled upwards. Then he laughed, short and dry, more like a cough than a laugh.

'What's so funny?' I asked.

'Kate, you're a bit naïve at times. She's real crumpet, you know. There's probably half a dozen men in Longborough following her about.'

I thought about that for a moment. 'Hubert, she's scared. I mean really scared.'

'In that case,' said Hubert, 'she must know who he is.'

I'd thought about that too. 'Sometimes, Hubert, you can be annoyingly right.'

He grinned sheepishly and left.

I stared out of the window again. If she did know who this man was, why on earth wasn't she telling me?

I sat for some time alternating between doodling and staring out of the window. Then Hubert reappeared, framed in my doorway like some lost actor looking for the right set in a film studio.

'I've been thinking,' he said.

'That's good, Hubert.'

'There's no need to be cheeky.'

'I'll make you some coffee,' I said.

While I made the coffee Hubert too couldn't resist staring out of the window.

As I handed him a mug he said, 'I'm worried about this one, Kate. She's got a confident way of walking. She wouldn't be that scared over some bloke who just fancied her, would she? And has she been to the police yet?'

'Yes, Hubert, she has been to the police and no she would not be that scared of a mere...a mere...'

'Admirer?'

'Yes. And what do you mean about you being worried about this case? It's *my* case.'

Hubert's face assumed its crestfallen expression. 'I was worried about you,' he said. 'I was only joking about her being followed by lots of men. I mean this one could be a real psycho.'

'I'll go to the police if I get time, Hubert.'

'You could spare some,' he said. 'Just lately you've spent more time staring out of that window than trying to bring business in.'

'Hubert, do I tell you to go out and bring in more corpses?'

He shrugged and walked slowly towards the door, where he stood with one hand on the doorknob as if about to insult me and then do a runner. 'I do my best,' he said. 'I have to rely on fate. You could make more of an effort.'

'I'm trying,' I responded as he opened and closed the door behind him. 'And I can manage quite well on my own, thank you.'

I wasn't sure if he'd heard me and if he had, no doubt he would have smiled to himself. The trouble is, I could probably manage without Hubert's help but it wouldn't be half as much fun.

THE POLICE STATION in Longborough is tucked away on the outskirts of town, an afterthought, built in the sixties when Longborough was expected to expand to take what was known as the London 'overspill'. The locals had anticipated a crime wave but the wave was merely a ripple because the promised relocation of jobs didn't happen. Those who did come were wealthy Londoners looking for the isolated thatched cottage, stripped pine, Laura Ashley soft furnishings, Barbours, green wellies and a chance to hang their onions from the ceiling. The reality was that if no one comes to see you living in trendy rural isolation you can't show off your good taste or your magnificent onions and quite soon depression and homesickness set in.

I'd gleaned the crime statistics from listening to the regulars of the Swan pub who were experts on both past and present crimes and criminals. Crime, it seems in the nineties, has escalated to correspond with the emergence of the video shop as a new species of entertainment. Car thefts and joy-riding had replaced poaching as a night-time occupation and the occasional rampage had replaced the evening stroll. All this criminality was due to weird reading schemes in the first year of primary school or to single parentage or, and one old man was quite convincing on this, to the lack of home-cooked meals in general—and boiled cabbage in particular.

I stood outside the police station looking at the three-storey building and wondered how exactly the police occupied their time. One or two patrolled the streets, of course, but what on earth did the others do? Surely they couldn't be too busy to watch out for one of the local district nurses?

The desk Sergeant, overweight and with a head like a square block, was busy filling out a form and while he kept me waiting I looked round the office. A huge phallic-shaped cactus in an equally huge pot stood in one corner and on the walls framed pictures of haymaking and lakeside views were hung in tasteful groupings. It looked very much like an upmarket dentist's waiting room, and was nearly as quiet as Humberstones' chapel of rest.

'That's our new image,' said the Sergeant proudly as he looked up from his form and flashed me an all-purpose 'community' smile. 'How may I help you, madam?'

'I'd like to speak to someone from CID, please.'

'Wouldn't we all, madam. Wouldn't we all.'

'Inspector Hook if possible,' I said firmly, hoping a bit of name-dropping might be useful. It was not.

'He's in a meeting, madam. Quality Assurance—Man Management or Community Relations, I'm not sure which.'

'What happened to crime-busting?'

'That's old hat, madam, gone with *Dixon of Dock Green* and *Z Cars.*'

I was beginning to get a little irritated so I squared my shoulders, lowered my voice, and said, 'Would you stop calling me madam, Sergeant, and suggest whom I could see regarding a criminal matter.'

'No need to get shirty, madam,' he said. 'I'm only trying to keep the public informed about current trends.'

'I do read the *Guardian,*' I said with a weak smile. 'But I would be very grateful if I could liaise with someone.'

He grinned cheerfully. I'd cracked the language barrier! We were now speaking the same language. Liaise was obviously a key word.

'Our liaison officer is also in the meeting, madam, but if you'd care to wait?' Signalling with his open hand he showed the array of empty chairs.

'I'll come back,' I said. 'My name's Kate Kinsella, by the way, of Medical and Nursing Investigations.'

For a moment amusement flickered in his slightly bloodshot eyes, then he said, 'Well, why didn't you say you were in the same game, love? DS Roade is available. I'm sure he'd have a chat with you.'

'Thanks. Wasn't he invited to the meeting?'

The desk Sergeant smiled. 'We always keep someone available, stashed away in case of a crisis. Is this a crisis?'

'Could be, for someone I know.'

'Right you are, love. Come this way.' He lifted the counter flap and indicated that I should come through. He pointed out a door along a narrow deserted corridor where the only sound was the ponderous noise of very slow typing. 'Second on the left,' he said, 'marked CID.'

The door was open and DS Roade was mid-finger in his typing and with his free hand midway into a Mars bar. At the sight of me he dropped the chocolate as though it had become red hot and his mouth opened and closed in an expression of startled embarrassment.

'I'm glad I've found you,' I said.

He pointed to the chair in front of his desk, threw the remains of his Mars bar into the bin, crossed his arms and leaned back.

'What's the problem?' he asked in a resigned tone.

I sat there and tried to ignore his youthfulness and his acne and that he had begun to look at me with the same lusty fervour he extended to the Mars bar. His acne had worsened since I last saw him and I wondered if he was still troubled by indigestion.

'It's about Vanessa Wootten,' I said. 'The district nurse. She came to see you, I believe, about being followed by a man.'

DS Roade adjusted himself back into his chair, re-crossed his arms as if to say 'don't press me' and sat silent. I waited. I supposed he was just showing me who was boss. Eventually he said, 'We didn't think there was much in that story.'

'Who's we?'

'Inspector Hook and me. We think she's neurotic.'

I moved forward slightly and drummed my fingers softly on the desk. I said nothing.

'She is, you know,' he said as if I'd argued. 'If I were you I'd leave well alone.'

'How can you be so sure she isn't being followed?'

'I didn't say she isn't being followed.'

'Well then, why won't you help her?'

'Let's say we've had dealings with her before.'

'So?'

'She's trouble.'

'Detective Sergeant Roade,' I said, 'I know MENSA turned me down once but I can understand really simple explanations. If you talk slowly I'll probably catch on.'

'There's no need to be sarcastic,' said Roade, 'I was only trying to save you bother.'

'I like bother. It pays the rent.'

'Okay. Don't blame me. Miss Wootten is one of our regulars. She's rung us several times, lives with a weirdo called Sean, who beats her up and . . .'

'He's gone now. And that doesn't mean she was wrong about someone following her.'

'No, I suppose not. But the last time she was in here it was to make a serious complaint.'

'Of what?'

'Of rape.'

I swallowed hard and tried not to seem too surprised. 'All the more reason to believe her, I would have thought.'

'Yeah, but that's all she did—complain. She refused to bring charges.'

I was beginning to feel Roade had cleverly made me walk into a verbal trap.

'Why was that?' I asked. 'She must have had a reason.'

Roade shrugged. 'It seemed strange to me. She was in a right old state when she arrived at the station. Then she calmed down, said it had all been a mistake and that she was sorry.'

'Did she name the man?' I asked. 'Did she actually know him?'

Roade raised an eyebrow at me which I presumed meant he was going to enjoy telling me.

'She said she didn't see him properly because he wore a black mask but that she thought she knew who he was. We questioned him, of course, but the bloke accused had a cast-iron alibi.'

'Which was?'

'He was on duty at the time with a colleague.'

'A colleague,' I echoed.

'Yes, Miss Kinsella, another PC, both on police duty at the time of the alleged incident.'

It was my turn for my mouth to drop and for Roade to smile in triumph.

'Oh dear,' I said, trying to flutter my eyelashes in a suggestive fashion, 'I've agreed to take on her case and find the man. Perhaps I shouldn't have...' I tailed off, trying to sound a bit pathetic.

'Are you all right?' asked Roade. 'You keep blinking.'

'Conjunctivitis,' I answered quickly, but by now I was thoroughly put out. I knew Roade wouldn't give me the suspect rapist's name and somehow I had to make this visit worth while.

'I'll have to give her the benefit of the doubt,' I said. 'I promised her some help and I'll have to do my best. Is there any advice you can give me?'

Roade grew visibly taller in his chair. 'About surveillance?'

'Yes.'

'Simple really. Always let someone know where you are. If you're sitting in the car take something to eat and drink, and in this weather a blanket. It gets perishing just sitting in a car and at night you can't keep starting the engine. And last, but not least, a good torch.'

I stared at him. I was impressed. I had merely planned to sit in the car like some giant slumbering moth.

'Thank you very much, Sergeant Roade. You'll be an inspector in no time. You really have been very helpful.'

He smiled, embarrassed.

As I left the office he said, 'Don't tread on the wrong toes, will you. Vanessa Wootten may be neurotic but, and I'll tell you this off the record, the PC involved is an oddball and alibis can be faked.'

'I could kiss you, DS Roade.' I blew him a kiss and, before his face had completely turned a dusky red colour, walked out of the office.

THREE

SURVEILLANCE, I decided, is a posh word for being bored rigid. This was only my second day of observing Vanessa Wootten's daily round but it felt much longer.

At six a.m. I had begun surveillance on Vanessa's terraced house in Percival Road, Longborough. At first it was a novelty. I drank coffee from a Thermos flask, read yesterday's paper by torchlight and was more than grateful to DS Roade for suggesting the blanket. I couldn't remember ever seeing any TV or film detectives wrapped in a blanket in their cars but I suppose it's just not macho to admit you are halfway towards hypothermia.

Dawn seemed temporarily held up that morning; it was cold, grey and very dark. The two-up, two-down, Victorian houses stood flush with the pavement, sombre monuments to domesticity and gardenless to ensure total commitment to the railway or factory. Gradually, though, one by one the lights of the houses shone through the gloom.

Percival Road needed all the help it could get, appearing in the shadowy light like some hideous place caught in a time warp. I half expected men with ashen faces and cloth caps to appear, to hear the harsh call of the factory hooter. But now there were cars and satellite dishes and fancy curtains and I was watching number thirty-six to catch the man who might, or might not, also be watching thirty-six. The day before, Wednesday, I had followed Vanessa from home to the Health Centre and from there to fifteen patients scattered around Longborough and the villages. The only person following Vanessa Wootten had been me.

Even so, I told myself as I sat there in the freezing gloom, I was being paid. Every five minutes or so I scanned the empty cars and watched the few men who left their houses. The man who had been following Vanessa could, of course, have come from anywhere in or near Longborough but just as easily he could have been a neighbour.

The bedroom light at number thirty-six went on at seven a.m. The pink ruched curtains cast a reddish tinge that almost matched the blood red of the front door.

I continued to watch the street and the departure of various men and women between seven and eight, all of whom either got straight into their cars or walked slowly, and with what seemed like reluctance, towards the centre of Longborough.

It was just after eight when Vanessa appeared. She glanced to both left and right then got into her car and drove off.

Following someone isn't that easy. I strained to see her red Mini from behind two other cars that had managed to get in front of me. At least one was driven by a man but it was impossible to tell what he looked like. I did manage to memorise one of the numbers and at the traffic lights scrawled it into my notebook.

I guessed she was going to the Health Centre first, and it took the pressure off my driving, which was just as well, as it had started to rain and every so often I had to wipe the condensation from my windscreen, the heater in my car functioning, like me, only in spasmodic bursts.

Longborough Health Centre stands in the midst of a thirties council estate, incongruously modern, looking more like a wrecked ship than a symbol of the new-style NHS. I supposed the portholed windows gave that impression, together with the domes and turrets and the inside piping that lay bare across the roof space like internal rigging. The captain of this craft, Dr Hiding, I knew slightly, and that's how I wanted the situation to stay. His brand of medicine was so heavily laced with religious fervour that unless your condition was immediately obvious, such as a severed leg, you were likely to get a prescription for prayer and, if you were really lucky, a massage as well.

It was here Vanessa collected her messages and the names and addresses of any new patients. I waited in the car park, running the engine occasionally so that I could use the windscreen wipers and then see well enough to take down a few car numbers, more for something to do than because I had a particular suspect in mind.

After about fifteen minutes she reappeared, head down against the rain, walking fast towards my car. As she approached I wound down the window,

'Hello, Kate,' she said. 'I've got a new patient in Farley Wood and two others to see there this morning.'

'Fine,' I answered. 'That's where I live. We'll be able to have coffee and chat.'

Vanessa smiled wanly. 'Sorry, Kate, have to be a short one, I'm really busy today.'

That annoyed me a little. She was paying me well, not that I'd seen any money so far, but she seemed so... uninterested, as if by acquiring me she now had some lucky talisman that would protect her from...nameless, faceless chummy.

AFTER VANESSA had seen her last patient in Farley Wood it was her turn to follow me. My cottage sits in a row of four houses opposite the imposing St Peter's Church and a triangle of village green in which one small oak tree stands. In the summer it's a pretty place but in the winter it is stark and forbidding and the tombstones I can see from every window in my cottage stare back at me; made worse by the fact I now know a few of the names of those who lie within the church walls.

Vanessa seemed impressed by my view and she stood gazing at the church from my front window for some time. I got the idea, though, that she wasn't so impressed with the general state of my cottage. I do have a frantic clean-up every three weeks on average, but housework is so repetitive, it's like having sex with a longtime, well-known partner. You think to yourself—well, that's it till the next time. And the next time it's still the same.

I left her standing at the window, while I went out to the kitchen and made instant coffee and arranged chocolate biscuits on a plate.

'Thanks,' she said on seeing the biscuits. 'I'm starving. I always eat more when I'm worried. Not that I put on any weight. I'm just lucky, I suppose.'

Did I imagine it or did she give me a pitying look? I ate my share slowly, not wanting to appear greedy, and consoled myself with the thought that I didn't have to do anything I didn't want to do—including dieting and boring surveillance.

'Have you made your hospital appointment yet, Vanessa?' I asked.

'I go next week,' she answered with a brief smile before she turned and stared out of the window once more. 'On Monday.'

Neither of us spoke for a while. I wanted to ask her tactfully about her pursuer but could come up with nothing better than a direct question.

'Have you any ideas at all who this man could be?' I asked.

She shrugged as she turned, then moved over to the sofa and sat down, her hands clutching her knees.

'I may as well tell you,' she began reluctantly. 'There is someone I suspect . . .'

So Hubert was right. 'Why didn't you tell me this before?' I asked.

'I don't know,' she said, 'I really don't. In a way I suppose I want someone to find him but I don't want to know who or why. Can you understand that?'

I nodded but I didn't really understand. 'Tell me about him,' I said.

She looked straight at me then and smiled sadly. 'I told the police all about it but they didn't believe me. I told you they think I'm neurotic.'

'Are you?'

'A bit,' she said with an apologetic smile.

I smiled too. 'Everyone's a bit neurotic about some things,' I said, 'especially if they are under stress. Take your time, Vanessa, and tell me what happened.'

She shrugged and stared down at her hands for some time.

'He raped me . . .' she whispered.

'Go on,' I said.

'His name is Paul Oakby. Some time ago I had an affair with him. It was very passionate I suppose at first, but it didn't last long. He became really possessive, wanting me to give up friends, even suggested I should give up my job. He suspected I was meeting all sorts of young attractive doctors. After a while things got worse and he began to accuse me of having an affair. He scared me. Anyway I broke off with him and he took it quite well. Sean moved in with me later. About six months ago I came home early from a party on my own. I'd gone with Sean but he'd got drunk and began to get very aggressive so I'd walked out...' She paused then and covered her face with her hands as if trying to blot out the memory.

After a few moments I said quietly, 'And then what happened?'

Vanessa removed her fingers from her eyes but kept her hands cupping her face. Her eyes flickered over me briefly and then she looked away. 'I opened the front door,' she continued, 'and went straight upstairs to the bedroom. I didn't notice anything unusual at first. I walked into the room and then the door slammed behind me. He was waiting there. His hands went straight to my mouth to gag me...I couldn't scream, but I kicked and struggled... I really did try to fight him off. But he was too strong. He forced me on to the bed and raped me... it didn't take long... he didn't speak ... and then he left.'

'It was definitely Paul Oakby? You saw his face?'

'Yes,' she said quietly, lying to me with her eyes shining as bright and true as the blue stained-glass windows in a church.

'And this is the man who you think is following you and wants to kill you?'

'I'm not sure.'

'Why wasn't he charged with rape?'

Vanessa's top lip trembled slightly. 'I couldn't face testifying. I just couldn't face it. I knew he'd come up with an alibi and I couldn't have coped with all those questions about my private life, especially as we had once been lovers.'

'I think I'd have felt the same, Vanessa,' I said. 'But what puzzles me now is why he should be following you. After all, you did him a favour. You didn't press charges and he lost nothing.'

Shaking her head she said, 'I don't know, unless he's mad.'

I watched Vanessa for a few moments. She could have coped with most things, I thought, and she lied convincingly. But she couldn't fake the sudden pallor of her skin or her obvious depression, or even the fear that seemed to lie buried within her and which surfaced occasionally to flicker in her eyes.

'Let's talk about the man following you,' I suggested. 'If it's Paul Oakby and he's still in the police force, surely he wouldn't have the time to follow you around. If he was on duty he would have been quite distinctive in uniform and you told me before you couldn't recognise the man but he was all-round average. How average is Oakby?'

'How...' she began, 'how did you know he was a policeman?' I didn't say. 'You're confusing me. I...I haven't seen him properly but who else could it be?'

'I'll have to be honest, Vanessa,' I said, feeling like a real snake in the grass. 'I've already been to the police. They told me about Paul Oakby; well, they didn't actually name him, but they did say he was a policeman. I just wanted you to tell me your version of events.'

'What do you mean my version? Don't you believe I was raped? Do you really believe I would lie about something like that? If you believe that perhaps you shouldn't be working for me.'

'I'm sorry, Vanessa. I sort of suspected you weren't quite telling me the whole story. I didn't want to waste my time or yours. After all, there's been no sign of anyone. Perhaps the man has realised I'm watching and has given up.'

Vanessa gave me a tight little smile before standing up and walking over to the window. Pulling my red mock-velvet curtains aside, she stared silently towards the church.

'Please, Kate, just give me a few more days,' she said, not turning her head. 'That's not much to ask. I'll pay extra.'

'It's not just the money,' I said hurriedly, 'although I could do with paying for these two days...'

'I've got it with me. Sorry I forgot to give it to you before.' She spun round to face me. 'It's here, look!'

From her uniform pocket she handed me a bundle of fivers. At first I wanted to refuse, money often giving me irrational guilty twinges as though somehow I didn't deserve any. But then I noticed her eyes filling with tears and I nodded.

'Okay. A few more days,' I said reluctantly. 'That's all I can promise at the moment.'

She smiled with such obvious relief that I felt guilty once again for even thinking of abandoning her.

'Thanks a million, Kate. You won't regret it.'

I knew then that I was bound to.

'I must go back to the Health Centre now,' she said. 'Why don't you have a break and meet me there after lunch?'

'Are you sure?'

'It's not far,' she said. 'And I know you'll be along later.'

I shrugged. 'You're paying, Vanessa. You're the boss.'

As I showed her out there was just one thing troubling me. 'The night you were raped?'

'Yes?'

'How exactly did Oakby get into your house?'

She pursed her lips slightly, with anxiety or confusion, I wasn't sure which.

'He didn't break in,' she said slowly. 'I think he had a key. I lent him mine once but he gave it back. Perhaps he had another one cut.'

'And you didn't think to have the locks changed?'

'I'd forgotten about it, Kate. Really I had.' She smiled then, so sweetly, that just about anyone would have forgiven her just about anything.

That smile unnerved me a little. 'It was just a thought,' I said.

I watched as she started her car and I waved as she drove off. My hand was still in mid air when, from the pathway alongside the church, a dark green car slowly followed hers. A man was driving, but I couldn't see his face properly as he wore a cap pulled low over his forehead.

I tore into the house to get my car keys. I'd managed to register some of the number plate: VMS 2.

Well, Mr VMS 2, I'm coming after you.

It's a pity he didn't know because he might have felt as uneasy as I was beginning to feel. Not just uneasy but scared, because to remember the letters of the car number plate I fitted words to them. VMS stood for VERY MAD SOD.

FOUR

WE DROVE SLOWLY in convoy on the winding road towards Longborough. It was a case of having to, because Vanessa's Mini was stuck behind a tractor. The green VMS in the middle of the sandwich, which I now recognised as an elderly Chevette, kept his distance from the red Mini but I kept close up his rear, partly to get the rest of his number plate and partly to get a better look at his face. The one reasonable glimpse I did manage confirmed that he was far too young to be wearing a cap.

At the traffic lights I was left behind and when I arrived at the parking bay in front of the Health Centre Vanessa had already parked and VMS, bold as a naked bum, had parked beside her. I parked my multi-ownered, purple resprayed (to cover the rust) Ford opposite both of them. Then watched as Vanessa got out of her car and VMS wound down his window and they began chatting. After a few moments she waved to me and shouted, 'See you at two, Kate.'

VMS had now closed his window and was staring towards the Health Centre and making no plans to go anywhere. Even though he obviously posed no threat to Vanessa I still wanted to know why he was hanging around. After ten minutes I could stand it no longer and I walked towards him and knocked on the side window of his car. Startled, he wound down the window.

'Excuse me,' I said, trying to be polite. 'Could you explain why you followed the red Mini here?'

'What?'

He had a mouth so small he must have found cleaning his teeth a struggle and a beaky nose that plunged downwards to meet his tiny oral orifice. If he had a girlfriend he could only have managed to kiss her sideways on.

'You seemed to be following the red Mini.'

'Did I?' he asked.

'You did.'

Nervously he pushed his checked cap a little back from his forehead and stared at me with eyes the colour of stale porridge. 'I don't know what you're talking about,' he said. 'I've come to see the practice nurse. She hasn't arrived yet, her car's not here. I hate hanging about in the waiting room, everyone hacking and coughing, so I sit here for as long as I can—it's a lot healthier. But I certainly haven't been following anyone. I just drove here today as I've done twice a week for the last month, once to see Dr Hiding, once to see the practice nurse.'

'Oh dear,' I said. 'What's wrong with you?'

'This,' he said, as he pulled off his cap and revealed a balding head with a few downy fair hairs sprouting amongst a mass of pustules.

'That's nasty,' I said. 'Is is getting better?'

'Not so you'd notice,' he replied. 'It's defying medical science at the moment. But I live in hope.'

'I'm sorry to have disturbed you. I hope it gets better soon.'

He nodded and as he did so I remembered where I'd seen a similar nose—the Reverend Collicot, vicar of St Peter's. So this was the son known in the village shop as, 'Young Christopher—poor soul.' I now realised it was his looks the customers referred to, not, as I'd thought, because he was at theological college. Vanessa, of course, would have known him from his frequent visits to the Health Centre. No wonder she was unperturbed by his presence. The vicar's son was hardly the Very Mad Sod I had anticipated, more he of the Very Mouldering Scalp.

I couldn't help wondering why Vanessa wanted me out of the way for the rest of the morning but I felt like a break from sitting in the car and I wanted a chat with Hubert. He kept an ear to the ground in more ways than one and I wanted to tell him about my visit to the police.

On the way to Humberstones I saw there was a free parking space outside the bakery and I couldn't resist stopping. The novelty of being able to park directly outside shops hadn't waned yet. I'd lived in north London for many years and felt lucky if, there, I could manage to park my car outside my own home.

I chose two fresh cream meringues because then I could tell Hubert that they were lower calorie than most of the other cakes. He was always saying he's watching his weight but really I think he's watching mine. Anyway, I knew he had a sweet tooth and when he saw the cakes he wouldn't exactly smile but his face would fall into creases of pleasure.

Hubert's hearing as always seemed very acute because he came to the foot of the stairs as soon as he heard me open the side door.

'You've had a phone-call this morning,' he said accusingly.

'Cream cakes!' I said, ignoring his tone and the phone-call and waving the pink ribboned box before his eyes.

'Haven't you heard of healthy eating, Kate?'

'You mean lettuce and lentils. It's not the same, is it, Hubert? They don't wrap up half so prettily. I'll eat them both if you don't come up and share them.'

It was then that his face began to crease and I knew I'd won.

Between mouthfuls, we sat opposite each other on the dove grey office chairs Hubert had bought me after my last major case and I told him about Vanessa's mysterious rapist and showed him the two hundred she'd given me in fivers.

'Is she on the game?' he asked.

'She's a district nurse!' I protested.

He shrugged. 'There's a lot of it going on. Especially in Percival Road.'

'How do you know she lives in Percival?'

'You wrote it in your diary.'

I guessed that Hubert was wondering how she could afford me so I said, 'When someone pays cash in a shop the shop assistant doesn't say, "Excuse me, madam, but how can you manage to afford this?" do they?'

'I suppose not,' agreed Hubert grudgingly. 'But I wouldn't want you to get involved in anything dangerous or illegal.'

'No need to worry about that,' I said. 'I've got a feeling this one is just going to die on me.'

'What you need is a bit of inside information,' suggested Hubert. 'Someone else must have seen her being followed, some old biddy she visits must have clocked this bloke. After all, Longborough isn't a large place, it's not New York where an oddball would go unnoticed.'

'You're right, Hubert, I've been to New York, and crime there lurks just like London fog in those old B pictures. In this country prospective criminals hide away pretending they're as innocent as the characters in *Coronation Street*—'

'You're getting ever so cynical, Kate,' interrupted Hubert. 'And when did you go to New York?'

'I'll tell you about it one day,' I said. 'But you are right, Hubert, I do need to be on the inside. Perhaps Pauline could fix me up with some relief work.'

Pauline Berkerly, a friend of mine, ran the Berkerly Nursing Agency and she usually managed to find me work without asking me too many questions about why I wanted it.

Hubert continued to nibble his meringue while I rang her.

'District work?' she said, sounding doubtful. 'That's usually well staffed; people don't want to work in hospitals any more, you know. Your only hope is if they have some long-term sickness. I'll ring you back if I hear of anything.'

As I put down the phone I remembered the other call. 'Hubert, who was it who called?' I asked.

Hubert got up to go, his expression glum, and walked towards the door. The electric light was on and my new white paper shade seemed to highlight the shiny bits of his black suit. When Hubert looked miserable, I thought, and in certain gloomy lighting, he only lacked the scythe to be my idea of the all-purpose Grim Reaper.

As he opened the door he said, 'A Paul Oakby rang— nasty, aggressive character. He said he'd keep ringing till he got you.'

'Sounds ominous,' I said and I knew that Hubert knew that the smile on my face was false.

I spent what was left of the morning planning how best to interview a suspected rapist and wondering who let it be known I had an interest in him. Only the desk Sergeant and DS Roade knew I had been to the station. I hoped it was the desk Sergeant.

For lunch I ate four naked cream crackers, drank two mugs of fully caffeinated instant coffee and at one o'clock I watched Hubert walk off down the High Street towards the Swan. If I was around we usually went together. Perhaps he was sulking, I thought, or maybe he was going to meet his ex-wife, whom he met regularly at the pub to give her maintenance money she in no way seemed to deserve.

Either way, I'd have to think of something to have my name re-entered into his good books.

JUST BEFORE TWO I drove to the Health Centre. Vanessa was waiting beside her car.

'I thought you weren't coming,' she said, touching my arm as if for confirmation I was there in the flesh.

'I wouldn't let you down, Vanessa. Was there any sign of him this morning?'

'None at all,' she replied. 'You must have frightened him off.'

'Let's hope so.'

I didn't mention Paul Oakby's phone-call, not wanting to upset two people in one day.

Her first stop was Little Charnford, a hamlet to the west of Longborough.

It was a right-hand turn out of the Health Centre and at the first gap in the traffic Vanessa was off, leaving me to wait, and by the time someone stopped to let me go, the red Mini was out of sight. I drove on, soon out of Longborough and on to empty country lanes. A wintry wisp of sunshine poked occasionally through grey clouds but I knew that in a couple of hours it would be dark and I definitely wanted to be somewhere other than these rural depths before nightfall.

The first suggestion that Little Charnford even existed was a near-collapsing signpost opposite a single-track road which said 'Village only' and then underneath, 'Little Charnford 4 miles'. Four miles! It seemed more like six. Especially as I had to leave the car every few minutes to open gates and then close them again. It was obvious that Little C belonged to an estate: it bred sheep like other fields grew wheat and had more 'Private' signs than Longborough had traffic lights. Eventually, though, I arrived at the small cluster of measly, run-down, thatched cottages that comprised the hamlet.

Vanessa's red Mini couldn't be missed, it was the only car. The cottages, a group of six, formed a semicircle around a patch of scrubby grass and a feeble elm tree. I parked alongside her car and waited. And waited. I got out of the car and walked around her car. More to be nosy than because I wanted to stretch my legs. I'd read somewhere that personality showed itself in the interior of cars. I didn't like to think what torn upholstery, chocolate wrappers and the odd apple core said about me. The inside front of the red Mini was immaculate. A box of tissues and a first-aid box sat neatly in the glove compartment. She even had a fire extinguisher. The back seat was equally tat-free but a rumpled tartan blanket covered the upholstery, which surprised me. I would have expected it to be folded.

Having inspected her car I sat back in mine, switched on Radio Four and listened to an earnest lady talking about the joys of living in Lapland. She wasn't at all convincing. After that there was a totally incomprehensible play. I kept looking at my watch. I bet she's having tea and home-made biscuits in there, I thought. But which cottage? At three thirty I realised the play would continue to be beyond me and I decided to join Vanessa with an offer of help and the hope of joining in with the tea and home-mades.

I knocked at the cottage immediately opposite her car. After some time the door opened, bringing with it a waft of damp mustiness and an equally damp and musty-looking elderly man.

'What do yer want?' he said.

He wore a pair of dark grey trousers, with grease patches down both legs, held up by a wide brown belt and above that a short maroon jumper exposing a scraggy neck that would have looked equally at home on a well-strangled chicken.

'I'm looking for the district nurse,' I said. 'She's in one of the cottages but I don't know which one.'

'She ain't here, me duck,' he said, shaking his unstable-looking head.

'Could you tell me where you think she might be?'

'She might be at Mrs Brigstock's or Mrs Harold's, both off their feet they are, been poorly a long while they have. Just waiting for us all to die he is.'

'Who is?' I asked.

'The owner, Duke of Croxly. It's his estate. I thought everyone knew that. You a townie?'

I nodded.

'Which cottage is Mrs Brigstock's?' I asked, thinking perhaps my best bet would have been to knock on all six doors.

'She's next door, duck. Daffodil Cottage.'

'Thank you. I'll try there.'

Daffodil Cottage was entirely without flowers. Weeds and dust and peeling brown paint and half the thatch replaced by green corrugated metal were its only decorative features. The front door had deep cracks down the wood and one of those old black latches, a reminder of the days when it was safe to leave doors open. Mind you, that was probably because no strangers ever came near. I don't expect they could even find Little Charnford.

I knocked loudly. There was no reply. I waited and knocked again. Suddenly the whole place gave me the shudders. The old people here had been buried alive. There was no church, no shop, no school, no living souls to be seen at all. I knocked again and shouted 'Vanessa' and 'Mrs Brigstock' alternately at the top of my voice. I'd chosen the wrong cottage. Mrs. Brigstock was either asleep or stone deaf and if Vanessa had been there she could not have failed to hear me.

I was about to give up and try another door when I found my hand unable to resist the novelty of that black latch. I lifted it and slowly opened the door. Inside it was as dark as a cave but narrow and low as a tunnel. To describe this area as a hall or a corridor would have defied even the most flamboyant estate agent. It smelt of boiled cabbage but not freshly boiled and of the same musty damp I had smelt next door.

Calling out 'Mrs Brigstock', I moved towards the first door on my left. This is the living-room, I told myself but I hesitated with my hand on the latch of the door; for I had the feeling that there wasn't a lot of living going on inside.

FIVE

THE LATCH clicked open and I pushed the door ajar very slowly, in the hope, I suppose, that any shock I might receive would be assimilated equally slowly. The smell of foetid air mixed with wood smoke rose towards me like vapour. And after the smell it was the sounds I noticed most, the ticking of a clock and the barely perceptible sound of someone breathing.

As the door opened fully I could see the bed on the left-hand side of the room. Facing me was a curved black headboard and beneath it the unmistakable sight of a dead old lady. Strands of silver-white hair lay, like down, on her forehead and under her chin had been placed a lace-edged pillow. All that seemed to cover her was a white sheet and in the sea of white she had become almost indistinguishable from her bedclothes. In contrast the blackness of the headboard made it look like a gravestone for a corpse that had already been prepared.

By the small front window on a wicker chair sat Vanessa. She didn't move as I came into the room, her eyes staring straight ahead, dull and blank.

'Vanessa,' I said softly, but there was no response. That she was in shock was obvious. But why? Finding dead people is an occupational hazard for district nurses. So why on earth did Vanessa look as if she'd caught a glimpse of hell?

I knelt down in front of Vanessa and touched her hand. She flinched.

'What's wrong?' I asked.

She stared ahead for several seconds then she turned her head sideways. I followed the movement of her head. A mirror, circa 1950, hung above the grate that contained the ashes of a wood fire. I looked again at the mirror; something was written in what appeared to be a black felt-tip pen in its top left-hand corner. I walked over, stood on tiptoe and read the words written in small capitals: FOR YOU. V.

It was then I took my first close look at the corpse. I removed the pillow from under her chin. My impression of white sheets was correct, for that was all that covered her. Her arms were laid neatly by her sides, as if, as if— someone had already laid her out.

'Did you—touch her?' I asked.

Vanessa shook her head. The dead woman's face had deceived me too, for although as white as any paper shroud, under her eyes were tiny blue haemorrhagic patches. The pillow beneath her chin had not only kept her jaw closed, it had smothered her as well.

As if reading my mind, Vanessa said dully, 'There's no phone.'

'I'll stay here,' I said. 'You know which houses have a phone. Go and ring the police.'

As if in slow motion, she stood and walked towards the door, gazing blankly ahead of her. I watched as she went outside, past the front window towards the third cottage in the row. I doubted somehow that she would come back and the police would take at least twenty minutes to arrive. That would give me enough time to explore the house.

I walked the short distance to the closed door at the end of the narrow hall, guessing the room beyond to be the kitchen, a euphemism for this poky area. One curtainless filthy window about a foot square stood just above a grimy butler sink with a single cold tap which dripped relentlessly into a half-filled enamel bowl. Dripping taps irritate me and I'd placed the bowl on the wooden draining board and was about to empty it away when I realised I'd probably just wrecked a perfectly good clue. I'd have to explain my fingerprints away, but at least I was beginning to know a clue when I saw one.

A few dirty plates were stacked on the top of a low brown cabinet covered with old Fablon, curling at the edges, and next to them a Belling electric cooker. A whistling kettle half-filled with water was on one ring and solid porridge in a saucepan on the other. Both were cold to the touch. The cabinet contained a packet of cornflakes, a half-full bag of sugar, a packet of oats, a bottle of Camp coffee, four full packets of sweet biscuits, a tin of condensed milk and half a bottle of sterilised milk. There was no fridge or sign of any fresh food. There was no sign either of a forced entry. The back door had not been forced and the glass in the window remained intact.

Upstairs there were two bedrooms, one bedless, both with the musty smell of rooms left closed and unused, and a bathroom with an ancient enamel bath over which loomed the spout of a geyser, grey with age and lack of use. It was fairly obvious the occupant had long since stopped making the journey up the narrow steep stairs to either bedroom or bathroom. But where, I wondered, did she wash or do anything else?

Downstairs again, I found the answer. The wicker chair Vanessa had sat upon was a well-disguised commode and in a sideboard I found a washing bowl, soap and towels and the nursing notes, nowadays known as care plans. The dead woman's name was May Brigstock, she was eighty-four years old, suffering from a multitude of ills but alert and able to state that she wanted to die in her own bed. That she had achieved and by the expression on her face, death had not been that unwelcome, or come as much of a surprise.

The district nursing service had visited twice a day for many months, a neighbour had provided food at lunchtime, but at night she had been alone. As her condition had deteriorated Vanessa had been asked to call early afternoon as well. From the notes it seemed Vanessa visited on the days off of the district nursing sister, someone called A. Caltrop.

I stood by the bed and touched May's face. It was as cold to the touch as a can of lager from the fridge. I guessed she had been dead some hours although now I had become aware of the coldness of the atmosphere it wasn't surprising her face felt cold. By her side on a low wooden table an alarm clock, green and yellow, ticked on loudly; cheerful, and relentless. By its side on the low wooden table stood her bottles of tablets and a full glass of orange squash covered by a paper tissue.

Whoever had killed her hadn't been clumsy or had tidied up afterwards. The tablets were varied: a diuretic, analgesics—mild, glycerol trinitrate for angina and digoxin to control her erratic heartbeat. It was really only the diuretic that interested me. Diuretics increase the output of urine and are always taken first thing in the morning. That meant I would have to inspect the commode and feel the bed if I was to make a calculated guess about the actual time of death.

At that moment I heard the police car draw up and I thought I'd have time to have a quick peek in the commode. I managed to open the lid of the chair to find the plastic lid and bowl underneath. It was empty. I then tried to replace the seat of the commode chair but it slipped to the floor. As I bent down to retrieve it I heard heavy footsteps, but it was too late, I was caught—incommoded. And that was how I felt and looked.

'What the hell?' said the square-faced man who entered the room first. He looked rather like an extra from a *Godfather* film, black-haired and swarthy, attractive, if you like the type who wears a gold bracelet with his name engraved on it and expensive mohair suits. Not that he wore either, but they would have suited him. Instead he wore a dark brown belted raincoat with matching brown shoes and on his face a hint of designer stubble.

'What's going on?' he demanded.

I had two options, I thought: I could either lie or tell the truth. I lied. 'I felt faint,' I said, trying to sound pathetic. 'I only tried to sit down but the seat lid fell off.'

There was no offer of sympathy forthcoming and now I became aware that DS Roade and DI Hook were crowded into the tiny room and were sending me signals of gloat. I attempted to smile at both of them. Even if they were gloating I did at least know them, and in the past they had tolerated me with an amused detachment. This CID person I suspected was the new broom at Longborough police station, the last senior CID man having been pensioned off with the DTs some months before.

'Did you find the body?' asked Mafia-man.

I shook my head. 'The district nurse found her—Inspector?'

'Detective Chief Inspector,' he said tersely. 'Finbar O'Conner. And your name?'

I told him.

'I hope you haven't touched anything else,' he said. 'You bloody country people are all the same. Anyone would think you never read a crime novel or watched the box. There's always someone who has to have a poke around.'

Finbar O'Conner was an angry man. Obviously a conscript and not a volunteer. Now I knew he was Irish and not Italian I half expected to see a twinkle in his brown eyes. But Irish eyes obviously weren't smiling today so I put a hand to my forehead and hoped I looked pale and wilting. I certainly wasn't going to admit to touching the bowl in the kitchen. My acting ability didn't strike any chords though, because all three now surrounded the bed, and I was left in the middle of the room like the last weed in the garden waiting for the chop. It came soon enough. I heard Hook whisper something about private detectives and the surly Superintendent turned angrily.

'You,' he said disparagingly, 'can go. There's no space here for hangers-on. Once the Scene of Crimes people get here plus the police surgeon we won't be able to scratch ourselves in comfort. Where's the person who found the body?'

I looked towards the window about to point them in the right direction when I saw the red Mini driving away.

'Well?' he said.

'Well,' I said slowly, 'she appears to have just left.'

'Get after her,' he shouted at Roade.

I had to admit he was decisive.

Roade shrugged and looked at me as if somehow I were to blame. He rushed out of the cottage and I mumbled, 'I'll be off then.'

O'Conner looked up from the corpse. 'You do just that. We'll be in touch.'

As a CAR CHASE it had been a non-event. I'd had trouble keeping up with Roade but as far as I could see he was speeding for the sake of it, for Vanessa's red Mini seemed to have disappeared. I imagined she had found another route to Longborough or she had managed to give Roade the slip by taking a different direction entirely. Either way, it seemed she was determined to get away. But why? If she wanted evidence of persecution then surely this was it. Or was it? I thought about that as I drove along Percival Road looking for her red Mini. I didn't really expect to find it there, but it pays to do the obvious first—well, in theory anyway.

Humberstones' car park seemed active as I drove in. Two men were giving the hearses the once-over although Hubert doesn't like the word 'hearse', he just refers to them as the 'Daimlers'. Both men gave me a cheery wave with their polishing rags as I walked in the side entrance. I had one foot on the stairs when I heard a whispered 'Kate'.

Vanessa sat, or rather crouched, on the jumble sale chair. My eyes hadn't quite accustomed themselves to the half light but I didn't need to see her well to be aware of her fear: I could almost smell it.

'The police are after me,' she said, looking at me as pleadingly as a dog desperate for a walk.

'Not all of the police,' I said, 'just DS Roade and I suspect he'll be here any minute. You'd better come up to my office.'

She followed me up and although my office needed a light on I left it gloomy in the faint hope that Roade might suspect I was out.

'I had to get away. I just had to,' Vanessa was saying as I peered out of the office window to the street below. 'I couldn't face their questions. When I feel better I'll talk to them.'

'Yes. Yes,' I said distractedly, expecting to see Roade's car zoom up at any moment.

'You're not listening to me.'

Turning reluctantly from the window I said, 'I am, Vanessa, but I'm trying to plan what to do next. Have you got any ideas?'

'I could hide here, couldn't I?'

'Well you could, but it would have to be very temporary. The police must consider you a very important witness—you did find the body after all.'

She nodded. 'Where shall I hide?'

'I'll ask Hubert,' I said.

Hubert surprisingly didn't ask any questions but he did give me the benefit of one of his 'Are you sure you know what you're doing?' expressions. I flashed him a confident smile but he wasn't convinced and merely scowled in response.

'Put her in the chapel of rest,' he said. 'There's a large cupboard in there.'

I had to admit I'd never noticed a cupboard, but then coffins tend to dominate the eyes in such places.

I led Vanessa down the stairs and into the chapel but really it was a case of push and shove. Anyone would have thought she was going to the gallows.

'I'm claustrophobic—I don't think I can go in a cupboard,' she said as we entered.

'You'll have to stand behind the door, then,' I said, 'and hope he doesn't come in.'

I was beginning to get a little irritated but the sight of the chapel was surprisingly soothing. One covered coffin stood before an oak table on which stood a silver cross on a white circular cloth. Light from a high stained-glass window mottled the table and sparkled on to the silver cross. And everywhere there were flowers and bowls of pot pourri, perfuming the air like incense.

'Oh God,' murmured Vanessa.

'I won't leave you here long,' I promised. 'I'll fob Roade off and he won't want to miss the action. He'll be rushing back to the scene of the crime as fast as he can.'

Taking Vanessa by the arm, I had to push her behind the door and position her reluctant body. Her unease seemed to be filtering through to me and now I noticed how grey her face looked in the muted light, but it was her mouth that worried me most. Her lips moved as though she were talking to someone. For a moment I stared at her and it was as if I saw her for the first time. And suddenly I wasn't scared just for her. I was scared for both of us.

SIX

'JUST HANG ON, Vanessa,' I urged, but she didn't seem to hear me and I thought about bundling her into my car and driving off, somewhere—anywhere. But then I heard a car draw up and I guessed it was Roade. I tore up the stairs, threw open a file on my desk and tried to look casually inert, even though my respiratory rate would have done credit to an eighteen-stoner doing their first 500-metre sprint.

Hubert opened the door to Roade and in deeper tones than usual announced, 'Detective Sergeant Roade is here to see you, Miss Kinsella.'

'Thank you, Mr Humberstone,' I mumbled with my hand over my mouth, trying to disguise my heavy breathing and keep myself from laughing.

He glared at me and said, 'Mr O phoned again.'

Hubert was, I thought, trying to get me rattled. I continued to breathe deeply, only too aware of the rise and fall of my undersized breasts, which I refused to restrict with a bra, just in case one day they might start to grow.

'Thanks for letting me know,' I said.

Roade strode in then, looking round the room sulkily like a four-year-old who'd just had his Plasticine model trodden on by the kid next door.

I smiled with as much charm as I could muster, while Hubert shut the door with a bang.

'Hello, Sergeant,' I said. 'Do sit down. Have you found my client yet?'

'There's no need to be funny. I know she's here somewhere. She's left her car in the town centre. I don't know what you're playing at, but we'll have you both down the station if you're not careful.'

'Please sit down,' I repeated. 'I do know where she is.'

'You do?' he said as he sat down.

'I do.'

'Where is she?'

'I said I knew where she was but that doesn't mean I'm going to tell you—yet.'

Roade tightened his tie with slow deliberation as if it were around my neck and then he leant forward in his chair and tried to look menacing. It didn't work. Youth, acne, and a face not much bigger than a teacup meant he just looked slightly put out.

'*When* are you going to tell me?'

'I'm not trying to be difficult,' I said. 'It's just that Vanessa Wootten is still in shock. She's being followed. A murder, it appears, has been done on her behalf, she's made a recent suicide attempt, and all in all, she's a wreck.'

DS Roade shrugged as if to say none of it was his fault. 'We've still got to speak to her.'

'Of course you have but I hope you'll agree to my suggestion.'

'Which is?'

I didn't answer for a moment and once he had relaxed back into the chair I knew I was winning.

'We'll come to the police station tonight,' I suggested. 'She'll be calmer by then and she can make a proper statement. Vanessa does need protection you know—'

'From herself more like,' interrupted Roade.

'What's that supposed to mean?'

He stood up. 'You'll find out,' he said. 'Just make sure you do turn up though, because O'Conner will have my nuts pegged out on a washing-line if you don't.'

'We'll be there, I promise.'

By the heavy thump of his departing footsteps he wasn't too pleased to be returning to Little Charnford *sans* Vanessa but I was delighted. Perhaps now, I thought, Vanessa would open up to me and I could begin to acquire a list of possible 'admirers' or just possibles. Including the most possible of all—Paul Oakby. As soon as I heard Roade's car drive away I went to the chapel of rest.

'He's gone, Vanessa,' I called. 'You can come out now.' I opened the door gently and peered behind it. Like standing on a drawing pin my brain got the message immediately but my mouth took a second to engage sound. 'Oh, shit!' I shouted, which I thought was restrained in the circumstances.

Hubert came rushing along the corridor. 'Keep your voice down, Kate. I've got grieving clients in the office.' Hubert was talking in his downstairs voice, a serious, almost sanctimonious whisper.

'She's disappeared,' I answered, in a furious whisper.

'Well, there's no need to swear in the chapel.'

'Shit is not a swear-word, Hubert, it's only slang. I promised the police I'd take Vanessa to the station tonight and now she's run off—'

'I can't talk now,' interrupted Hubert. 'I'm in the middle of selling one of my most expensive packages. My business is very competitive, you know. I could lose them to the Co-op.'

All the whispering seemed to have calmed me down. 'Sorry, Hubert, I just don't know what to do next.'

Hubert was silent for a moment but then he took my arm and led me towards the side door. 'Either,' he said, 'she's gone back home, or she's gone back to work just as if nothing's happened.'

'I had thought of that, Hubert,' I said quietly. But then in a loud voice that I hoped would carry to his office I called out, 'Thank you so much, Mr Humberstone. You really are the best funeral director in town. I'll be sure to recommend you.'

He was only slightly amused and he practically pushed me out into the courtyard, where I stood coatless, wondering exactly what my next move should be.

After a few moments I began to shiver and I thrust my hands into the pockets of my favourite baggy green cardigan, drew it around me and then walked quickly to my car.

I decided I had three options: I could attempt to find out who her patients were for the afternoon and try to find her on her rounds; simply drive round aimlessly looking for her, or, and the most obvious of all, see if she had yet returned home.

I was driving back towards Percival Road thinking how selfish my client was being to go missing and put me in a very poor light with the CID when I realised... missing... She was *missing!* Disappeared, gone, abducted, kidnapped?

The side door of Humberstones was always open during the day. Perhaps she had been followed through the town and HE had simply snatched her from behind the door. By the time I'd parked my car outside the Health Centre I'd begun to change my mind, though, for it seemed very far-fetched. Surely she would have struggled, made some sort of fuss. But then she was already in shock and perhaps she had tried to scream but no sound came. It was no good guessing, I told myself. I would just have to find her.

I DROVE FIRST to number thirty-six Percival Road and knocked very loudly on the door. There was as much response as if I'd been knocking on Hubert's cold-room door. Then I did a swift tour of the town centre but could see no sign of any abandoned red Mini.

Finally I decided to see Vanessa's immediate boss. The Assistant Director of Nursing Services (Community), Frederic Tissot, sat in a box-like office with a large rubber plant on the floor next to his desk and a squash racket propped up in one corner of the room. On his desk were an assortment of papers, two phones and a photograph of a wide-eyed pretty woman with an equally wide-eyed baby. Was it an affectation to have family photos on a desk? I wondered. Did it make a statement about working long hours, so long that you forgot what they looked like, or was it merely a form of boasting. This is my wife and child—aren't they beautiful? Either way it made me uneasy about Mr Tissot.

He'd stood up as I entered; he was fractionally taller than the rubber plant and as brown as its stem. He wore a fawn-coloured suit and a shiny cream shirt that made his eyes appear darker in contrast. His features seemed as neat and newly pressed as his clothes. When he spoke, his voice had been steam pressed too, with a French accent, which if I had closed my eyes I would have found incredibly sexy. I didn't close them, I just listened carefully.

Not that he said much. When I explained my presence and that I was a Registered General Nurse his first words were a muttered, 'That girl!' He paused then, to rearrange the papers on his desk and smile at me. 'Has a very bad sickness record. She is a little unstable, you know. Very emotional.'

'Well, she did find a dead body this afternoon.'

Tissot shrugged and I noticed that his cream shirt was pure silk, like his accent. I explained that it was murder and that she was being pursued.

He seemed to find that funny. 'Ah! Vanessa has that effect on men. She is very attractive.'

'Perhaps I'm not making myself clear, Mr Tissot. I believe Vanessa Wootten is in great danger. She's my client and it's my job to find her and protect her.'

'Of course, of course. But you must understand I have all my community staff to worry about. With Vanessa...absent...we will have to find a replacement. At the moment we are very overburdened. Winter is a time when we have many deaths and twice the caseload we have in the summer months.'

'You don't seem very concerned about one of your nurses being in danger, do you?' Sexy accent or not this little man was beginning to irritate me.

'Miss Kinsella, if you knew the whole story,' he said, 'I'm sure you would not say that. We have tried very hard to be supportive to Vanessa. She seems to have a penchant for violent men and a psychiatric history.'

'What does that mean?'

'It means,' he said, 'that your client has had to be hospitalised twice.'

'What with?'

'Depression, paranoia. She seems to be deluded that there is a man after her, although no one else has seen him. That's very odd, is it not?'

I nodded. Of course it was odd. But then she would have been the only one knowing he was there. The only one scared enough to be always on the alert. If her colleagues only half believed her story they would be less than rigorous in watching for him.

Eventually I managed to persuade ADNS Tissot that Vanessa could well be visiting her usual afternoon patients and if he could give me their names and addresses I would be able to find his district nurse and perhaps even manage to keep her working. That suggestion seemed to do the trick.

'Everything will soon be on our new computer,' he said proudly. 'But in the meantime we rely on lists. If you want I can probably manage to work out who she's likely to see on a Friday afternoon. We do have our regulars, of course, who have been on the books for years.'

The list didn't take long. She had five regulars and she always started with May Brigstock because she was the furthest out of town. The others were in Longborough itself.

'Be a dear,' said Frederic as I was about to leave, 'give Mrs Spokes her insulin injection if Vanessa hasn't been and tell the others I'll get a nurse to them tomorrow.'

'First or last for Mrs Spokes?' I asked.

'Last. Vanessa does her about five thirty usually. Ring me if you don't find her because I'll have to arrange cover. You do have a current nurse's UKKC card, I hope.'

'I don't have it with me. It's in my purse in the car.' Being on the Nurse Register and paying regular dues had its benefits.

'Don't worry, I can always check,' he said with a smile that bordered on this side of threatening. I looked at my watch. It was nearly five. Growing dark outside. And I felt exhausted.

I emerged from Tissot's office to find Dr Hiding waiting outside in the corridor, so near to the office door I wondered if he'd been listening. He could have been handsome with his regular features and thick dark hair, but he wasn't. His heavy rimmed glasses and habit of wearing cardigans gave the impression of an academic loosed from some dusty library. It was his eyes that spoilt his looks; those two grey orbs, the colour of mould on a dead mouse, peered at me.

'Ah! Miss Kinsella,' he said with satisfaction as he gave my shoulder a pat. 'How are you? I hear my patient Vanessa Wootten has engaged you—'

'I can't stop, Dr Hiding, but I would like to meet for a chat some time.'

His hand still rested on my shoulder and I gave a little shrug of irritation. He didn't seem to notice.

'Any time, my dear, any time. God willing.'

He made my flesh creep but I forced a smile. I used to feel that way about Hubert but in comparison to Hiding he seemed both normal and wholesome.

I found the first house on the list quite easily, and the second. Both patients complained bitterly that their nurse hadn't turned up but I promised them a visit the next day and was rewarded by offers of tea. I would have loved one but Mrs Spokes's insulin was due and by now I just wanted to find Vanessa and go home, have a hot bath and a large Scotch, preferably at the same time.

The third house I didn't find so easily. I had to ask directions twice and by the time I did find it I was shivering, miserable and my blood sugar and caffeine levels must have been at an all-time low. The man who answered the door looked in a similar condition. Of medium height, he had a slight stoop, was unshaven and his hair, thin and wispy on top, grew long and uneven into the back of his neck. I supposed he was in his sixties. He wore a well-creased lilac sweatshirt and faded jeans and the worn, anxious, defeated expression of the full-time carer. And it was obvious that I was a disappointment.

'Oh dear,' he said. 'I was expecting the nurse.'

'Do you need help? I am a qualified nurse.'

'It's Benjamin. He needs turning and changing. He's dying, you see. I would be most grateful...'

I introduced myself.

'I'm William Beige,' he said, and he stretched out the word Beige, so that at first I hardly recognised it. 'It's not AIDS.'

'Oh good,' I answered, which was totally inappropriate but I couldn't think of anything else to say.

He led me along a dark hallway to a multicoloured beaded curtain which clacked back into place as we walked through. The room beyond the curtain was large but cluttered. In one corner a standard lamp glowed, casting its light on to the bed alongside it. Old newspapers, junk mail and a couple of cats lay haphazardly between lumpen brown furniture. Dingy antimacassars covered the three-piece. I guessed this had been the family home; the Edwardian atmosphere had not been re-created, it seemed original.

As I approached the bed William Beige kept close beside me.

'He had a stroke,' he whispered. 'Four years ago. He can't speak. I used to understand what he wanted but two weeks ago he became semi-conscious...he's dying now, isn't he?'

He wanted me to deny it but I couldn't. Benjamin lay towards me, twig-like wrists poking from beneath frayed pyjama sleeves and from his lop-sided mouth saliva had trickled down his chin and lay glistening like the track of a snail at the base of his neck.

'Show me where Nurse Wootten keeps everything and then I can manage on my own if you'd like to have a rest —you do look very tired.'

William declined. 'It won't be for much longer, will it?' he said, as his eyes filled with tears.

There was no answer to such a question. I put an arm around him and although I was sure he wanted to cry the tears dried in his eyes and he sniffed and patted my shoulder and said, 'We've been together a long time.'

Together we washed and changed Benjamin, turned, creamed and padded him. Then, painfully slowly, he managed to swallow a few sips of water from a spoon.

'He looks better now,' said William when we eventually finished.

But he didn't. He just looked more comfortable and cared for.

'I have to go now,' I said. 'Do you have a night nurse to visit?'

William Beige nodded. 'It was very kind of you to help. Please stay for a drink.'

I was about to decline but he said, 'Please. I hate drinking alone.'

So I stayed and drank two sherries. Midway through the first I mentioned Vanessa.

'Lovely girl. She's been so kind to both of us. Is she sick? She always seems so worried and nervy. I expect she has her problems, though. We all do, don't we?'

I nodded. He'd had four years of problems. Four years!

'Has she ever mentioned being followed?' I asked.

William shook his head. 'Not as such,' he said thoughtfully. 'But...well, she did always peep out of the windows before she left...as if...as if someone might be there.'

As I left I asked where Shakespeare Road was.

'Mrs Spokes's place?'

I nodded.

'Next road on your left. Now, *she* might be able to help you. She knows everything. What she doesn't know she embroiders. I think the nurses use her house as an unofficial office. They leave messages for each other.'

'Thanks, Mr Beige. I'll leave my car outside your house for the time being.'

He smiled and waved and went back to his lonely vigil.

The two large sherries on an empty stomach had bucked me up quite well but the temporary euphoria faded as I realised how cold it had become. It was so cold that I ran to Shakespeare Road. It wasn't far enough for me to get warm and I stood shivering on the doorstep of number six praying for Mrs Spokes to let me in to the warmth of her house.

It was a road a little similar to Percival although here the houses had front gardens and privet hedges. Number six had a weedy garden and a brown front door but the red shaded light that glowed behind the curtained front window seemed to offer a certain cheeriness.

Mrs Spokes took a long time to answer and as she walked towards the front door I could hear why. She walked with a limp, the pronounced sound of a leg being dragged along.

'You're . . .' she stopped, surprised.

I was surprised too, for Mrs Spokes seemed to have been caught in a time warp—just past the Second World War. Her hair was still brown but she wore it in a roll, the size of a plump sausage around her neck like a half collar. A hair clip held what would have been a fringe in place, and the whole creation was further secured by a hair-net. Her eyebrows had been roughly pencilled in

black and thick powder tracked along her wrinkles to the
smudged red lipstick on her lips. Her full-length, cross-
over, floral apron was worn on top of a short-sleeved
cotton dress, also with flowers.

'Who are you?' she asked suspiciously.

I told her and thought how easily I had been allowed
into the three other homes. Not one had asked for proof
of identification.

'Come on in, then,' she said. 'Better bloody late than
never.' I wasn't sure if she meant me or the insulin.

'Where's Vanessa?' she asked as I followed slowly behind her to the room I presumed was the kitchen. 'She off
sick again?'

'She's just delayed,' I said.

'Huh!' answered Mrs Spokes angrily.

The room we entered was the back room with a small
kitchen attached. A table, covered with a fringed maroon cloth and a piece of embossed white plastic, was laid
for one, with a knife, fork, sauce bottle, cup and saucer
and the *Sun* newspaper. There were two straight-backed
armchairs and a large black and white TV that was on,
but with the volume turned down. A gas fire roared at
full therm, making the room quite hot enough for a cotton dress. There were no pictures on the wall, or mir-
rors, or knick-knacks.

'Sit down, then,' said Mrs Spokes, pointing to the
dining-table chair in front of the knife and fork.

I hesitated. 'Your insulin?'

'I've waited this bloody long I can wait a bit longer.
You're not in a rush, are you?'

'Well I...'

'Fry-up be okay? I've got some lovely smoked bacon.'

I protested that I hadn't come to eat her food.

'I cook for all the nurses. Who else have I got to cook for? You just sit there and read the paper. It'll only take a minute.'

I opened my mouth to protest again but she had already limped into the kitchen and soon I could hear the sound of sizzling bacon. And once the smell drifted my way protestation became impossible.

Within minutes the plate was put in front of me. Two rashers of bacon, fried egg, mushrooms, tomatoes and a slice of fried bread.

'Well, get on with it,' she said. 'Before it gets cold.'

'What about yours?' I asked.

'I'll have mine later. I don't eat in front of people.'

I was glad I didn't have that hang-up. The food tasted wonderful, especially washed down with hot sweet tea. And as I ate Mrs Spokes sat in her armchair watching the silent screen and talked and talked. First about her 'aggreephobia' then about the other patients on the patch, about how she couldn't and wouldn't give herself the insulin injections and finally about Vanessa.

'She's a daft little madam. She's been here many a time for a chat about her blokes. She can't seem to pick a good 'un. Once we had a right carry-on here. One of them came here to the house, banging on the door for her. I wouldn't let the bugger in and Vanessa did a runner over the back gate.'

'When was that?'

''Bout two years ago now. I think that was the last she saw of him. Thank Gawd.'

'Did she ever tell you she thought she was being followed?'

'Course she did. Never stopped going on about it. I always keep an eye out for her, though.'

'And have you ever seen him?'

Mrs Spokes shook her head. 'He's too clever for that. He uses different cars. He's like a bleedin' ghost.'

It was after seven when I finally gave Mrs Spokes her insulin and made it clear that I really had to go.

'Where's your coat?' she said.

'It's in my car.'

'Where are you parked?'

'Just round the corner. It's not far.'

'At Bill and Ben's?'

I didn't catch on immediately. 'Yes,' I said.

'How are they?'

I shrugged.

'Here, you take this,' said Mrs Spokes as she handed me a bottle green coat. 'Go on, put it on.'

I desperately hoped no one I knew would see me in the coat but the night air was so cold I was grateful to be warm. I was just thanking her and waving good-bye when she said, 'I've seen that car before.'

I spun round to see a black car moving slowly into a parking position opposite. At first I couldn't see the driver's face but then he looked directly across at me and gave me a slight nod.

His skin shone in the muted light of the streetlamps as though he were sweating. Then I realised it was merely the glow of Frederic Tissot's unnaturally brown skin.

SEVEN

'WHO IS HE?' Mrs Spokes asked, so loudly that in the quiet of the night her voice seemed to carry like an echo.

'It's Fred,' he answered before I had a chance to open my mouth. 'Don't be alarmed.'

'What you doing round here?' she yelled as Frederic started to cross the road to join us.

He answered as he got to the kerbside. 'I've just come to give a message to Miss Kinsella, that's all. You go on back in the warm or you'll get cold.'

Reluctantly Mrs Spokes turned to go. 'Right,' she said, 'I'm off. Don't forget to come in for a drink, though, Fred. You haven't been round here in weeks. I'm surprised you know what your staff are up to.'

We both watched silently as she limped with painful slowness into the house.

'I've been everywhere looking for you,' he said. 'I thought you'd have finished here ages ago.' As he spoke a mixture of sherry and garlic hit the back of my nose. I must have grimaced because he noticed.

'Bill and Ben's,' he explained. 'I've been there over an hour. I thought Ben was near to death at one point but then he rallied. Bill collapsed weeping and I had to stay.'

'Why were you looking for me?'

'Mr Humberstone rang. He's got a message from the police for you and he was worried. What took you so long?'

'Mrs Spokes,' I answered.

'Did you eat the lot?' he asking, smiling and showing perfect white teeth.

'I did. It was delicious.'

'That's very good,' he said. 'She feels a great insult if people don't eat her food. With luck I'll be offered tea and toast.'

'*Bon appétit,*' I said, smiling, hoping my teeth looked as good as his.

As I walked back to my car clutching Mrs Spokes's old green coat around me, I thought—what the hell am I doing? My client's gone missing, probably kidnapped, and I'm wandering the streets on unpaid nursing missions when I should have been looking for her. I should at least have rung the police and told them exactly how she disappeared. Now it seemed they were after me.

Driving towards Humberstones I began to think that eating the eggs and bacon had been a major sin. Perhaps, while I'd been tucking in to my fry-up, Vanessa was tied up somewhere, unfed, ill-treated. Even dead.

The High Street was deserted, a few bits of litter lifted from the ground as flurries of early March wind caught them and then dropped them again. The sky was black and clear and on such a night it would have been easy to think Longborough had been evacuated. Apart, that is, from the pubs. As I passed them and saw their cheerful bursts of light and heard wisps of laughter, I found them reassuring. The Swan, with its splendid thatch, attracted an older population than the Cock and Hen, mock Tudor, and second home for bikers and tall under-age drinkers. Both pubs, eventually, I supposed, provided business for Humberstones.

At first I thought Hubert had gone home because the whole of the ground floor was in darkness but then I looked up and noticed my office light was on. Hubert was obviously lying in wait for me.

'You've got no consideration,' he said, his face flushing an unattractive pink colour. 'I've been hanging around here for hours. You've had enough time to...well you could at least have rung...' He paused long enough to register the coat. 'And why are you wearing old rags?'

'I thought it was quite fetching.'

He ignored that. 'The police rang. They want you to ring back. And Paul Oakby rang again. He says he'll be in the Swan tonight.'

I sank on to one of the office chairs in utter weariness. 'This is all getting too much for me, Hubert. I couldn't find Vanessa and I had to see her patients. I'm beginning to get really worried. I seem to have let her down before I've even started.'

'It was her fault, she ran off,' said Hubert.

'But did she? He could have sneaked in and got her.'

'We would have heard if she'd made a fuss. I would have heard, anyway.'

'Perhaps she couldn't make a fuss. Perhaps he held a knife to her throat.'

'Stop being so dramatic,' said Hubert irritably. 'I'm hungry and I want a pint. I've had a bad day as well. Two interments and one cremation is no joke, you know. I've spent most of today with a glum face.'

'Glumness suits you.'

'That green coat suits you.'

I was tempted to throw it at him but I resisted the urge, took it off and put on my own black quilted one, which I kept meaning to replace because it made me look like a tea-cosy on legs. But it was obviously an improvement because Hubert managed a smile.

'Come on then, Hubert,' I said, 'let's go and smell the barmaid's apron. I'll ring the police from the pub.'

The Swan was full of good cheer, tobacco fumes, the smell of beer and burning logs, and little red lamps that spread a cosy glow over heads and faces like some heavenly aura. I sat in an alcove well away from the crowded bar, rested my head on my hands and closed my eyes.

'The place is full of big feet,' said Hubert as he placed a brandy and lemonade in front of me and stood to have his first few sips of beer as though he couldn't wait until he sat down.

'Big feet?' I queried, thinking Hubert totally obsessed with the subject.

'Fuzz. Bobbies. Police.'

'Where?' I said, turning my head to look at the male throng around the bar.

'Everywhere.'

'Did you see one with a small spotty face, looks about twelve?'

Hubert shook his head, while I carried on searching for a back view I recognised.

'No need to ring them now,' said Hubert. 'They can give you the message personally.'

I shrank back in the chair and into the shadows. 'Let's get out of here, Hubert. They might have a go at me about Vanessa not giving them a statement. I couldn't bear it.'

Hubert raised an eyebrow as if to say I must be joking and then said, 'Drink up, Kate. I'm having at least two pints and I've ordered a bar snack and I'm not going to miss that. Anyway, it's not like you to be timid. Besides, they already know you're here.'

'How?'

'I told them.'

'Why?'

'They asked.'

'Oh, very funny. Thanks, Hubert.'

'There's no need to get cross. Someone was bound to recognise me in here. It is my local and I am quite well known.'

'You'll be mayor next,' I said and was amazed when he seemed pleased with the idea. His lips gave a definite twitch at the sound of the word mayor. I took up my drink, downed it in one, shrugged at Hubert as if to say, 'Call me timid would you?'and advanced towards the bar.

At first I didn't see DS Roade but suddenly he was there in front of me, bursting through a group of be-suited men.

'Kate,' he said happily as if I were a long-lost buddy. His spots showed less in the red glow, and then I realised . . . he really was red, and drunk, very drunk.

'Come on, girl,' he said, 'you come over here. Mr O'Conner wants to have a word with you.'

He grabbed my arm and pulled me into the throng. It was how I imagine a midget would feel in a rugby scrum. My eyes were at chest level with most of them and the whole atmosphere was so overwhelmingly jolly and masculine I felt like ducking and running. Someone else took my arm and squeezed it. It was Finbar O'Conner, Chief Inspector.

'Not much muscle there.' He laughed. 'Not for a private detective.'

Everyone seemed to think that hilariously funny and I had to turn my head away to avoid the whisky fumes that escaped from his mouth like dragon's breath.

'Piss off,' I said quietly.

'Tut. Tut. You naughty girl.' He clamped an arm round me and half turned me, which was just as well because I was quite taken with the idea of kneeing him.

'A drink for the lady,' he shouted to no one in particular but a voice called back immediately, 'What does she want?'

There was more guffawing.

'Double brandy,' I said loudly.

Within moments the drink was passed through to me. I looked at the large amount of brown liquid, wondering if I should try downing this lot in one. I decided against it. What would that prove?

As I took the first gulp I noticed a man watching me. He stood at the far side of the bar, a little away from the general crush, one hand holding a pint glass, the other supporting his chin. I got the impression the others accorded him his own personal space. Through fear, I thought, and not respect. He had cold blue eyes, a thick nose that could have been broken once or twice, a low forehead, and a pugnaciously jutting lower jaw. Not a particularly ugly man—but aggressive-looking. 'A nasty aggressive type' were Hubert's words and I was sure he was Paul Oakby and, rapist or not, I didn't like the look of him.

'We're celebrating,' a voice behind me said. I turned my head which was the only part of my body I could move with ease. It was Inspector Hook, with bloodshot eyes and more grey-looking than I remembered him. He suffered from migraine. No doubt he'd have one on the morrow.

'Celebrating what?' I asked.

'Getting a result and our new Chief Inspector's arrival and the fact . . . that the CID beat the woodentops at five a side.' He enunciated each word with the utmost care.

The police were, I thought, very much like nurses—any excuse for a celebration, although nurses usually kept to cheap vino and a low profile. Longborough police were obviously more blatant with their boozing.

'Result?' I queried casually.

'The murder.'

'Which murder?'

'We don't have that many. Today's murder.'

'May Brigstock?'

'That's the one.'

He slurred on 'that's'.

'Explain it to me, Inspector,' I said. 'I've had too much to drink.'

'Haven't we all. We think we've got the killer.'

'Really?' I wasn't surprised. I was amazed. 'Who?'

'Mr. Brigstock—Brigstock's nephew, and our best suspect so far. Nasty little tyke. House-breaker, mugger, car thief. He's... adaptable.'

'He certainly is,' I said. 'This is a first-time murder, I take it?'

'Are you being funny?' he asked, squinting at me as if he could tell my state of humour by peering at me through slitted eyes.

'Perish the thought, Inspector. I'm just eager to know more. Is he in custody now?'

'He will be as soon as we can find him. We can definitely nail the little sod—his fingerprints were all over the house.'

'I expect mine were too,' I said, but he didn't seem to hear me. So I asked, 'And the writing on the mirror? Is that his usual modus operandi when he's nicking things?'

Hook looked at me stonily. 'That message was for his aunt.'

'But it said "For you. V."'

'Ah!' Hook said triumphantly. 'That was for Vera.'

'Who's Vera?'

'Vera May Bri... Brigstock, known as May.'

I tried to keep the surprise from my voice and my face. 'And you're sure it was him?'

Hook nodded. 'Sure we're sure. We wouldn't be celebrating, would we? You're not convinced though, are you? Neither was your little friend.'

'Little friend?'

'Vanessa Wootten. She came to see us this evening, about six. Gave us a good statement. She was still a bit upset but she said a few days with her sister in... Derbyshire would sort her out.'

I smiled, as if I already knew, and murmured something about the pretty countryside. But I felt angry and disappointed. What was she playing at? All that worry and she was quite safe and swanning off to act out her victim role with her sister. Well, I'd been manipulated long enough.

Hook, noticing perhaps that I'd lost interest, began to force his way through to the bar again and I searched round for the comforting sight of Hubert's balding head. I couldn't see him and as I turned back I saw that thick nose was making his way towards me through the crush with a raised beer in one hand and what seemed to be a brandy in the other. He was flashing me a leery expression as though by buying me a drink he was hoping for something in return. I looked around again for Hubert. He was nowhere to be seen. I turned back. Thick nose was already by my side now, smiling as he handed me the brandy. And the smile was as slick as a scorpion's tail.

EIGHT

'PAUL OAKBY I presume?' I asked in what I hoped was a casually cheerful tone.

'The same,' he said, the smile vanishing. 'Let's find somewhere a bit quieter to talk.'

He took my arm as if he were arresting me and led me over to a two-seater table by the exit.

'Where's your minder?' he asked as he guided the chair under me.

'Minder?'

'That weird undertaker.'

'Mr Humberstone you mean. He's my landlord, that's all.'

Paul Oakby smirked. 'Same difference.'

I didn't argue. 'Don't let's waste each other's time, Mr Oakby. Why exactly did you want to see me?'

'I thought you wanted to see me,' he said. 'Making enquiries, weren't you?'

'Well, I...yes. I was making enquiries about Vanessa Wootten and the...the rape. She suspects she's being followed, you see and I—'

'Alleged rape,' he interrupted, 'alleged rape. Get your facts straight, Miss Would-be-detective.'

'Look, Mr Oakby, if you're going to take this tone then I think there's no point in us continuing. I don't have any real interest in whether or not you raped Vanessa. That's past history now. I just want to find and stop the man who is supposed to be following her.'

'Okay. Okay. No need to get on your high horse. I'll just tell you this. I didn't rape her that night or any other. I don't need to rape women. They beg me for it.'

I raised an eyebrow. 'Really,' I breathed.

If his tongue had been forked he would definitely have given me the two-pronged attack. Instead he said, 'You bitch,' quietly, with such cold anger that I couldn't maintain eye contact and I turned my head to look once more for Hubert. This time he was back in his seat, raising his glass to me in cheerful salute.

Some time passed before either of us spoke again. Oakby continued to drink his beer with one hand clenched tightly around the handle and with his free hand he drummed on the table with his fist, slowly and rhythmically. I decided then that PC Oakby had to be humoured even if I had to grovel, for I only had him and Sean on my paltry list of suspects.

'Look, I'm sorry we've got off to such a bad start,' I began. 'I know hardly anything about Vanessa and I really would appreciate your help.'

He finished his beer and placed the glass carefully on a beer mat. 'What do you want to know?' he asked.

'Tell me about the suspected rape.'

'I was there that night,' he said, 'and you are the only person I've admitted that to. Tell anyone and I'll deny it. But I repeat, I did not rape her. We were driving round on patrol, Dick Hobbs and me. I saw Ness going into the house so we stopped outside and I dropped in to see her. A fleeting visit but she was pleased to see me. It seems she'd had a row with that pillock Sean and anyway, as I've said, she was pleased to see me.'

It took a while for me to understand what he meant. 'You mean you...you?'

'Yeah. We had a quickie.'

'With your colleague in the car outside?'

'He was happy enough. He read the paper.'

'I see,' I murmured, trying to sound as if having a quickie while on patrol was a normal part of police activity.

'You're shocked,' he said. 'You're more prissy than I thought, but then when I first met Ness I thought she was a prissy little bitch.'

'And now what do you think of her?'

'If you must know I think she's a raving nympho and she's nuts as well. She's been in the bin, you know.'

I nodded. 'I know she's had psychiatric treatment. I know too that she's very frightened. What I don't understand is why she should accuse you of rape.'

'Do nutters need excuses?'

There was no answer to that. Paul Oakby, I thought, was the worst type of policeman, no doubt over-endowed sexually but with an IQ not much higher than the average police dog and with less sensitivity.

'Another drink?' he asked.

I paused, drained my glass . . . why not? 'Thanks, I'd love one.'

I watched him push his way to the front of the bar and then talk to the men either side. I saw them turn and laugh and I grew hot and uncomfortable. The bastard probably thought he'd bought *me* for a double brandy.

When my drink finally arrived, it was a single.

'Let me give you some advice,' he said as he sat down.

'I could do with some,' I replied, trying to sound convincingly humble.

'Don't believe a word Ness tells you. She nearly ruined my career, you know. Dick's alibi that we stayed together saved my bacon. He knows what I'm like with women. I'll fight with any man but I'm not violent towards women.'

'And you don't hold a grudge against her?'

He mumbled something into his beer which I didn't quite hear.

'Could you say that again?'

His blue eyes stared at me for a moment. 'I still love the silly bitch,' he murmured. 'And that's the truth.'

And somehow I believed that it was.

I had only two more questions to ask. 'Do you always call her Ness?'

He shook his head.

'And do you know her sister's address?'

'No,' he answered, 'I didn't know she'd got a sister. She gave the impression she was an only child. Mind you, she didn't talk much about the past but she did have me looking for the someone who is supposed to be following her.'

I tried not to let the surprise show in my face, but he noticed.

'Take it from me,' he said, 'Vanessa imagines things. She believes that someone is following her. She believes I raped her. She doesn't deliberately lie but I think she's more than a little round the bend, don't you?' He smiled then, as if he were a small boy who'd got away with stealing from his mother's purse. A mixture of triumph and guilt.

I thanked him coolly and stood up to go.

And just when I didn't expect it he asked, 'She'll be all right, won't she?'

He sounded genuinely concerned, he even *looked* concerned, and at that moment I was sure I'd misjudged him.

'I'll do my best,' I promised.

Hubert looked forlorn sitting alone.

'You took your time,' he said. 'Want a drink?'

I shook my head.

'You'll drink with everyone else,' he said, peeved.

I was too tired to argue. I sat down. 'Another brandy then, Hubert.'

He smiled at his minor victory and walked off briskly to the bar.

'Vanessa's gone to Derbyshire,' I said as Hubert put a double in front of me, 'or so she says, to her sister's.'

'You don't sound convinced,' said Hubert.

'It just seems funny she didn't mention a sister to me or to Oakby when she was seeing him.'

That was my last coherent sentence before the brandy took hold. I heard a bell ring loudly for last orders and as it did so I felt like a boxer who'd gone down in round nine and was struggling to stay upright for round ten.

I vaguely remembered the walk back to Humberstones, stumbling as I walked up the stairs and then being helped on to the sofa-bed in the room adjoining my office. And Hubert tut-tutting at me as he took off my shoes and covered me with a duvet. It must have made Hubert's day, I thought, as the room began to dip and dive, and I said the common prayer of drunks everywhere: 'Never again, Lord, never again.'

I WOKE the next morning at seven with a terrible headache. I drank two mugs of strong black coffee, took two aspirins and waited for them to take effect. Then when my head no longer pounded, just ached dully like an old bruise, I decided to ring Vanessa. For I was sure she was at home. *Who* exactly was she trying to convince she had gone to Derbyshire, the police or me? But the phone remained unanswered, and I would have to go to her house to find out.

Vanessa's house in Percival Road showed no sign of life but there was a pint of milk on the doorstep. I gave a few raps on the door and as I stood waiting, I half turned towards the road. A small black van with those sinister dark tinted windows passed by. The only reason I noticed it was that it was going so slowly... so slowly, and suddenly I sensed that it was him, but by the time I realised, it was too late, he had speeded up and more traffic had followed on behind him. And I hadn't seen his face.

I rapped again on the door and shouted through the letter-box, 'Vanessa, it's Kate. Come on, open the door. I know you're in there.'

I didn't of course, but I guessed. A few moments later the door opened a fraction.

'Come in,' she said, hardly allowing me space to get through the door. 'I'm in the bedroom.'

Upstairs I had the same problem getting through the door. A chest of drawers had been positioned as a barricade and I had to hold everything in to get through. Vanessa's slim frame slipped through the gap as easily as a cat.

Once in the room I was surprised by its state. Clothes lay strewn over the floor, drawers were open, everything on the dressing-table had been knocked aside. Face powder and lipsticks and jewellery littered the floor.

'What on earth has happened?'

Vanessa's eyes swept around the room sadly as though she too couldn't quite believe it. She wore pale blue pyjamas that could have been silk, no make-up, and her eyes were red-rimmed with crying. She still managed to look wonderful.

'Did you see him?' she asked. 'Did you see him? He drove off when you arrived—in the black van.'

I nodded. 'I didn't see his face though.'

'Did you get his number?'

I shook my head. 'I wasn't to know it was him. Did *you* get his number?'

'No,' she said. 'He's too clever for that. He parked the van some way down the road in front of another car.'

She sighed heavily and slumped on the edge of the un-made double bed and then she began to tremble. I sat down beside her, put an arm around her and just patted her back until the trembling eased.

'Tell me what happened,' I said, 'slowly and clearly.'

She tensed and shrugged just a little. I removed my arm and she managed a weak smile.

'I'm sorry I ran out on you, Kate. I couldn't stand being in that chapel of rest. I felt trapped. I walked round for hours after that, just walked. Then in the evening I felt calm enough to go to the police. I gave them a statement. I told them I was going to my sister's in Derbyshire. Why I did that I just don't know. And then I came home...and found...' Her hand flicked towards the room.

'Go on,' I encouraged.

'He got in by breaking a pane of glass in the back door. He cleared up the broken glass but every room is a mess; he couldn't find it at first, you see. I'd put it on my bedside table and it must have fallen under the bed. And now he's got it.'

'Got what?' I asked.

'My work diary.'

I was about to say—is that all? And then I realised. A district nurse's work diary contains names, addresses, telephone numbers, times of visits. He could work out where she was at any time of the day.

'He'll know everything now. My patients could be in danger. He could be lying in wait for me...' Vanessa's voice rose to the edge of tears.

'Do you have MOEs in your diary?' I asked. Mode of Entry is how a district nurse gets into a house when a patient is alone or unable to walk.

'Yes,' she murmured. 'Only abbreviations but he could work them out, couldn't he?'

'Have you told the police about the burglary?'

'No, Kate, and I don't want them to know. They think they know who May's murderer is. Did you know that?'

'Yes. But when they do find him,' I said, 'I think they'll find they have got the wrong man.'

She stared at me for a moment. 'The police here aren't much good, are they?'

I agreed, but I didn't want her to lose complete faith in the Longborough constabulary. 'They don't have that much experience with murder, you know,' I said. 'Round here it's more likely to be drunks, kids stealing cars and the odd domestic. They are doing their best and you really must report this robbery.'

'No.' Vanessa's voice was quietly defiant. 'I just want *you* to be involved. You might be able to catch him if he thinks the police aren't on to him. He might get careless...'

At that moment the phone rang. We were both startled but the colour drained from Vanessa's face as though her blood pressure had just dropped thirty points.

'I'll get it,' I said as I lifted my arm to pick up the receiver.

Vanessa's hand cracked down on mine. 'Leave it,' she said. 'Let it ring.'

'But...' I began to protest.

'It's him,' she said, 'he knows we're here.'

It took a few seconds for her words to register. He knows we're here. We. We!

There was no doubt about it. He was after me too.

NINE

THE PHONE continued to ring, its harsh tones vibrating between us like an old and bitter recrimination.

'Why didn't you tell me he was ringing you?' I asked when it finally stopped.

Vanessa looked away as though embarrassed. 'He's only rung a few times, just recently. He says the same thing each time.'

'Which is?'

She paused for so long I felt annoyed with myself as well as her. Her caginess wasn't a trait I was used to in nurses and it made me feel distrusted. But I told myself to keep my mouth shut and eventually she'd tell me what I wanted to know.

'He says,' she began eventually, 'he says, "I love you, Vanessa. We'll be together soon...don't trust anyone. I'm always watching you." Then he rings off.'

'That's all?' I said, selfishly feeling thankful I hadn't been mentioned.

'That's enough, isn't it?'

'And he always gives you the same message?'

She nodded. 'There's no emotion in his voice. It's as if he's reading it.'

'What about his accent?' I asked.

'I'm not sure, Kate,' she said despondently. 'He doesn't seem to have an accent. He sounds like a machine.'

I wished he was a machine—I could short his terminals!

Vanessa broke the uncomfortable silence that followed with an offer of tea. I followed her downstairs and into her white and blue kitchen which was less cosy than an operating theatre and without the warm temperature.

'He didn't do much in here,' she observed, 'just opened the drawers. I try to keep everything tidy.'

The tea was made properly with leaves and a warmed pot and a tray with bone china jug and sugar bowl and cups to match. Hopefully I looked round for biscuits: there were none.

'We'll have tea downstairs, shall we,' said Vanessa. It wasn't a question.

The living-room was quite tidy considering books, all hard-backs, had been strewn over the floor. The furniture and furnishings showed Vanessa liked things to match. The autumnal leaf design in delicate gold and russet of the curtains was matched with the three-piece. A basket of dried flowers sat in an empty grate and on the low mahogany coffee table a bowl of oranges and tangerines glowed with a waxy tinge. Only the slight pink tones of the ruched net curtains jarred the room's colours; an incongruity like the huge earrings she wore the night I first met her.

'When we've had the tea I'll help you clear up,' I suggested.

'Thanks, Kate,' she replied, smiling with relief, 'I could do with a hand and I don't really want to be alone. Now that he's got my diary he can always be one step ahead of me. He's killed once, next time it might be my turn.'

There was no answer to that, so I turned my attention to my tea, wondering why it smelt old and musty like worn socks. It tasted even worse.

'It's Chinese,' said Vanessa, obviously misinterpreting my expression. 'It's so lovely and fragrant, isn't it?'

'It certainly is,' I said. 'Very...' I couldn't quite think of a word that described it. I swallowed the contents of the small cup quickly, grateful that she hadn't served it in a mug.

'Are you sure,' I said, 'that May Brigstock was killed by... him? As a murder it looked more like the work of Exit. I mean the police must have some reason for believing it to be the nephew.'

'It was him, Kate. It was *him.* No one believes me. Even you. I suppose you think I've done over my own house. You think I'm nuts, don't you? Did I imagine that black van? Did I? Did I?'

'No, of course not,' I said. 'Don't upset yourself, Vanessa. I saw it too. And what I also see is that, because you are so sure, you must have a very good idea who this man is.'

She sighed then and said quietly, 'Will you stay for a while, Kate?'

I assured her that I would and that we could spend the time tidying the house, and I hoped as we did so Vanessa would tell me more about herself than she had done so far.

We started in the bedroom, which took longer than necessary because we began chatting about our training and like nurses everywhere that meant the reminiscences went on and on.

'How about a drink?' suggested Vanessa. 'I've got plenty of gin and tonic.'

Two gins later I was beginning to wonder why I'd never liked the stuff before.

Eventually we finished tidying the lounge and we still had a half bottle of gin to go.

That is, until the phone rang again. I'd just come back in from washing up the cups when it rang.

'You answer it,' Vanessa said. She stood in the middle of the room staring at the telephone that rested on a small shelf by an armchair.

'You're sure?' I asked.

'Then maybe you'll believe me.'

I lifted the receiver and said nothing.

'Vanessa, I love you,' the voice began. A dull monotone, accentless. Disguised, I thought.

I still said nothing.

Then the voice changed to a whisper. 'If that's that interfering bitch from Humberstones you'd better get a slab ready for yourself. Don't think I'm kidding. I always get what I want. Leave Vanessa alone—she's mine.'

Then for a moment there was only the dull twirring of an empty line before I put down the receiver. I shivered but I hoped Vanessa didn't notice. I had to try and seem in control.

'I think you and I should stick together. Pack a bag and come and stay with me until this is all sorted out.'

She didn't answer at first, then she said, 'I'm not going anywhere. I'm staying here. I'm not moving.'

'We could have protection,' I said. 'Mr Humberstone could come to stay with us.'

She laughed. 'Honestly, Kate, I don't care if we have a military armed guard. I'm staying put. That's what he wants, don't you see? He could be watching the house now. Lying in wait. He could have a gun.'

'Why should he have a gun?' I asked.

'Why not?'

Why not indeed?

Upstairs again Vanessa sat on the duvet-covered bed propped up by matching peach-coloured pillows. I sat on the edge of the bed with a note-pad and pencil poised, feeling like a journalist just granted an interview with a reluctant actress.

'I'd like a list of men that you come in contact with,' I said, 'every male person. Milkman, shopkeeper, old boyfriend, even the postman.'

'That's ridiculous, Kate,' she said with a wry smile.

'No, it isn't. If he's out there, he knows you from somewhere, perhaps from the past, perhaps more recently.'

'What do you mean—if?'

I mumbled something about a slip of the tongue and then urged her to think hard.

Her hairdresser was male, not homosexual, her dentist was male, she knew a male nurse, her insurance man was male although she called him her financial adviser, her garage mechanic was male. The list of male contacts grew longer while my heart sank. I began to wonder if women in Longborough worked at all. By the time she got to the butcher and the postman, I too began to think this was a ridiculous list.

'Fine,' I said. 'Great list, Vanessa. That should give me plenty to start on.'

Would I ever finish, though?

'How about the ex-boyfriends?' I asked.

Her blue eyes stared at me and then she smiled. 'How far back?'

I knew then I was in for a long list. 'Five years?'

She nodded and closed her eyes. 'There's Sean of course, but it's not him and Paul . . . and . . .'

'Tell me about Paul.'

'He raped me,' she said flatly.

'He denies that. He said you were willing and that he still loves you.'

Propping herself on one arm Vanessa shot me a glance that would have stopped Genghis Khan in his tracks. 'You're very gullible, Kate, aren't you?'

I felt myself becoming hot. I knew that believing people too easily was one of my faults. But I consoled myself with the idea that there were people around who could even fool lie detectors. Sometimes intuition was all there was, and my intuition told me Paul Oakby, randy and aggressive though he was, had been telling me the truth.

'Let's not talk about Paul,' I said. 'The man following you you describe as of average height and build— Paul Oakby is well over six feet and heavily built. It's not likely to be him, is it?'

'No, it isn't,' said Vanessa miserably.

The gin and the phone-call had suddenly depressed us both.

'Let's get on with the list,' I said quietly and guiltily. The nurse in me felt I should be prepared to listen and counsel, but the rest of me wanted to be out and looking for him. The phone-call had finally convinced me he *did* exist and that Vanessa definitely wasn't a psychiatric case. Even so, I wasn't so gullible that I didn't know my client was keeping secrets from me, just as surely as a squirrel stores nuts.

Eventually I had a list of exes—Sean, Paul, someone called Ray Potten who she saw for about three months, and an Andrew Norten who she had seen about four times.

'That's all,' she said. 'In the last five years.'

'I'll have something to work on now. Anyone else you can think of before that?'

'Not really,' answered Vanessa uneasily. 'There's only my ex-husband . . .'

'What?'

'My ex-husband. He's happily married again now. We brought out the worst in each other.'

'Why didn't you tell me you'd been married?' I asked, trying to keep the irritation from my voice.

'It was a long time ago. I was divorced by the time I was twenty-three. Anyway he was a placid type, a bit jealous but not the type to follow me or make threats or... kill anyone.'

'Is he the type to hold a grudge?'

She shook her head. 'I've told you. He's remarried and very happy.'

'I'd like to talk to him though,' I said.

'You'll be wasting your time,' she said, shaking her head.

'Perhaps I'd be wasting my time anyway, Vanessa.'

'What do you mean?' she asked sharply.

'I mean that the only name you haven't given me is the right one, because I'm damn sure you know who this man is. What I can't understand is why you're protecting him.'

'I'm not,' she blurted. 'It's...it's...so difficult. I can't talk about it.'

'You're going to have to try,' I said gently.

She stared at me for a moment, her eyes glistening, then she turned her head and said, 'I do suspect someone but... he's someone from way back and—'

She broke off with a choked sob. After a moment she turned back and said huskily, 'I've been diagnosed as paranoid, you know. One psychiatrist termed me a manic-depressive paranoid. I've been taking tranquillisers for years. I was only allowed to do my district nurse training because someone at the top was sympathetic to people with mental disorders. You see, I've been followed by the same man for years and now he plans to kill me. He said he would, and although no one believes it, one day they will.'

'When you're dead, you mean?'

'Precisely, Kate.'

'Tell me about it.'

'I can't tell you all the details, it's just too painful and part of me says I could just be imagining things, but then I didn't imagine May Brigstock, did I?'

'You don't have to give me details if you don't want to, Vanessa, but give me his name and an address and I'll do the rest.'

'Oh, Kate, will you?'

'That's what you employed me for. The sooner you tell me who you suspect the better.'

'I don't know where he lives exactly but my sister will know.'

'Your sister in Derbyshire?'

'Yes. I haven't seen her for years and she doesn't want anything to do with me and she might not see you unless . . .'

'Unless I lie?'

'Well, yes. You could pretend you were a social worker or something.'

I smiled. 'I'm beginning to think even social work would be easier.'

Vanessa wrote down her sister's name and address and then she paused and spoke very slowly as though even his name had the power to affect her.

'His name is Colin—Colin Tiffield. There, I've said it,' she said, giving me a sad half smile. 'He's the most evil man in the world.'

'I'll find him,' I said. 'And I'll stop him.'

But my confidence was all show because Vanessa's words had made me shudder. And I didn't like leaving her alone but if I was to find him, then I had to.

'What about your job?' I asked as I picked up my shoulder bag.

'I'm off sick until he's found. I don't care about anything else any more. If he comes I'll kill him.'

'How?'

She lifted the pillow beside her to reveal a homemade arsenal: a carving knife, a rolling pin, a pepper pot, and some sort of spray.

'Do be careful,' I urged. 'He could use those things on you. If you hear anything unusual just ring the police. If you like I'll come back tonight. I'll be going to Derbyshire in the morning.'

'No... don't do that. You could ring me, though.'

I agreed I'd ring about ten thirty.

She stood up as I was about to leave. 'See yourself out, Kate,' she said. 'I'm going to barricade myself in.'

'You will eat, won't you? And get that window fixed.'

She nodded. 'I've got plenty of food in, I won't starve. You will remember I'm relying on you, won't you? I'm not leaving here until he's found or... until he comes to get me.'

'Don't say that,' I said, as a shiver like iced water trickled slowly down my spine. She was like the victim of a witch-doctor's curse and I knew that unless I found him quickly, by the time HE found her she wouldn't be in any shape to put up much of a fight.

TEN

As I LEFT I had the feeling I was being followed. I felt ashamed I hadn't had more sympathy for Vanessa. It unnerved me. It wouldn't have been so bad if I'd been sure. But I wasn't.

It started when I saw the black van just after leaving Percival Road. The black van stayed behind me until I got to the High Street. But not directly behind me, two cars back so that I couldn't see the driver, or the number plate. Even if I had seen the number would it have made any difference? If I was being followed it seemed that our man had a whole range of vehicles to choose from. Or was there more than one man? Someone paid to follow, someone like a . . . a contract killer.

I didn't tell Hubert. But he guessed something was wrong when he found that I'd run out of chocolate biscuits.

'What's the matter with you? No cream cakes, no chocolate biscuits? Have you gone on a diet at last?'

'No, Hubert. The investigation is beginning to take off. Food buying is taking a dive.'

'What investigation?' asked Hubert.

'I don't think that's very funny,' I said. 'I've got a definite lead now.'

'Oh good,' said Hubert, not sounding convinced.

To prove it I rang the Derbyshire number Vanessa had given me. There was no reply. But optimistically I said, 'I'll be away for the day tomorrow, Hubert. I'm off to Derbyshire; well, I will be if I can find someone at home.'

'I could come with you,' said Hubert, hope shining in his eyes as bright as religious fervour.

'Another time,' I said. 'It's only a tentative sort of visit to someone who might know where Vanessa's follower is living.'

Hubert shrugged. 'You're sure you've got the right man?'

'Well, I'm not absolutely sure,' I said, 'but Vanessa seems sure.'

'I thought she was convinced it was Paul Oakby,' said Hubert with some satisfaction.

'That's a different issue, Hubert, entirely different.'

'If you say so.'

Hubert positioned himself on the office chair opposite mine and stared for a few moments over my shoulder.

'You should have more than one man up your sleeve, Kate. Perhaps she's got it wrong; after all she's so good-looking it does widen the field quite a bit.'

'I'll find out tomorrow, Hubert, and I'll let you know. But if you want I can show you my list of men she does know.'

'Does know in the biblical sense?' asked Hubert with his usual hint of shyness when it came to sexual matters.

'Do you mean were they f...f...?'

'There's no need for that, Kate.'

'I was only going to say friendly.'

'Huh!' said Hubert, unconvinced.

'These are the men she knows,' I said, showing him the list.

Hubert gave a low whistle. 'I know one or two of these blokes—the postman and Jason the hairdresser, and Rajih Shah, the dentist. They all seem normal to me. What about her boyfriends?'

'Sean, her latest ex, has moved to Cornwall. Paul Oakby I've seen and I suppose that just leaves the two casuals and her ex-husband who lives in London. I doubt he makes regular sorties up here anyway.'

Hubert frowned. 'I didn't know she was married,' he said pointedly, as though I were deliberately keeping their nuptials a secret.

'Neither did I, Hubert, neither did I.'

'What's she up to now?' asked Hubert.

'She's not up to anything as far as I know. She's simply holed up at home, behind barricaded doors and with an arsenal of weapons under her pillow. She expects me to sort of pluck this man from the air...' I tailed off dispiritedly.

'Well now,' said Hubert, 'I've just had some news that might cheer you up.'

I bit back a retort about why didn't you tell me before and said, 'Yes, Hubert?'

'I've heard from my friend, in the morgue, that the police have come unstuck with their suspect, Mrs Brigstock's nephew. He's been crossed off the list.'

'It wasn't murder then?'

'Oh, it was murder all right, suffocation. But he didn't do it.'

'Come on,' I said when he paused, 'what's the punch line?'

Hubert smiled; he liked making me wait for bits of information. 'He couldn't have done it because... he was in a Glasgow prison doing time for burglary.'

'Oh,' I said. I was only slightly surprised. Even so, my stomach had lurched downwards and seemed to dance the tango with my uterus. 'So that means our...man...is definitely a murderer.'

Hubert peered at me, his thin neck pushed forward, his brown eyes glistening like sun on a muddy stagnant pool. I stared back at him.

'Why are you looking like that?' he asked.

'Like what?'

'You went all pale.'

'Hubert,' I said, 'I think he's after me too.'

His head sprang back as though pulled by invisible elastic. 'Right, that's it. I'm going to the police. They'll find the bastard—'

'But will they?' I interrupted. 'Vanessa's so-called paranoia hasn't just started. She was in hospital she...' I paused. The hospital—the psychiatric hospital! Where else would anyone expect to find obsessive psychopaths or social deviants...or potential murderers?

Hubert too caught on. 'You're not going to any mental hospital on your own, Kate.'

'Don't be silly,' I said. 'I've worked in them.'

'That doesn't mean much. How many times were you attacked?'

'Never,' I said, and it was true. I'd been very lucky. Anyway the majority of patients bordered on the timid and the more aggressive ones seemed to hurt themselves rather than others. I supposed that in the average mental hospital there were a few capable of murder but probably no more than in the general population of the supposedly sane. And of course the known criminally insane went to maximum-security hospitals.

'You're not going on your own,' repeated Hubert.

I didn't answer. I wasn't exactly planning just to visit, I hoped to work there.

Making Hubert a promise that I would keep him informed, he left to organise one of his more flamboyant funerals, what he called a 'black horse job'. And I rang Vanessa.

'I'm still here Kate,' she said. 'Has something happened?'

'No, Vanessa, nothing's happened. I tried ringing your sister but there's no reply. I can't go to see her unless I'm sure she's in, can I?'

'No, I suppose not,' said Vanessa. Then she added quietly, 'Someone followed you, Kate. Did you know?'

So I wasn't imagining it. 'Yes,' I said, 'but he's gone now.' I tried to sound casual because I didn't want to say that I felt that he was out there somewhere—watching and waiting. I changed the subject abruptly. 'Which hospital were you treated in for your depression, Vanessa?'

There was a long pause during which I had to check that she was still there.

'It was Pinetrees, in Tettering,' she murmured. 'Why? Do you think I need to go back in? I won't be a voluntary patient again, Kate, so please don't suggest it. They'll need a strait-jacket if they come for me.' Her voice lacked both conviction and passion; she was giving up, surrendering to the witch-doctor in her mind.

'I only wondered,' I said, 'because if I found out that Colin Tiffield wasn't responsible or had an alibi, maybe one of their ex-patients could be our Mr X.'

'It's a bit of a long shot, Kate.'

'You're probably right,' I said, fearing that it was indeed just that. Just before I rang off I asked, 'Did you get the window fixed, Vanessa?'

'Frederic is going to do it for me. He's putting up some plywood temporarily.'

'Good. I'll ring you tomorrow. Perhaps I'll have some news for you.'

'I hope so, Kate, for both our sakes.'

'I'll ring then.'

'Yes, do that. Bye, Kate and thanks.'

And she was gone. The line dead in my hand. My imagination was playing tricks on me, or was it? Her tone of voice had a sort of finality about it. I dismissed the idea as fanciful for what really mattered was that Vanessa was still alive and I had to keep her that way.

ELEVEN

THE NEXT MORNING I tried phoning Vanessa's sister again. There was still no answer. I sat for a while and stared out of the window. Bitter March winds were still blowing, chasing grey clouds across the sky, only to be replaced with more grey clouds. It was a good day for a funeral and when I saw the black horses arrive I knew I couldn't resist seeing them leave.

Hubert came up minutes later just to show off. He stood in the doorway in black tail-coat and a top hat with long black shiny ribbons. He smiled self-consciously.

'Do a twirl for me,' I said.

Obligingly he turned slowly and as he did so the ribbons drifted slightly as though in some final wave.

'Very impressive, Hubert. You really look the part. I'm surprised black horse funerals still take place.'

'There's been a revival,' said Hubert. 'For the rich of course.'

'Of course.'

'What are you planning to do today?' asked Hubert.

'I had planned to go to Derbyshire but there's not much point if her sister isn't there. Why is it life never works out as you plan it?'

'Nothing's easy,' he said glumly. 'It's all sod's law. You'll just have to do something else instead.'

'I suppose I could see Paul Oakby again. Perhaps I was wrong to have believed anything he said.'

Hubert looked at me sourly. 'You don't fancy him, do you?'

'Hubert! I'm surprised at you. I only meant in the line of duty, just for something to do. I like intrepid men, not rough diamonds.'

'I thought all women liked a bit of rough,' muttered Hubert as he turned to go.

'Funerals are your strong point, mein landlord,' I said, thinking I'd got the last word in.

But he had to have a parting shot. 'Pity detecting isn't yours,' he said.

The funeral procession left shortly afterwards which was just as well because it did take my mind off the problem of what to do next.

Hubert walked slowly in front of the four black horses. The carriage with the coffin trundled behind and the numerous mourners, all in black, walked three abreast behind the carriage. The wind whipped at Hubert's ribbons and at the horses' plaited manes, lifting them and dropping them in bursts that seemed to match the steady rhythm of their walk. A drum roll would not have been out of place.

Traffic and pedestrians stopped in Longborough High Street. Two elderly men removed their hats and bowed slightly as the coffin went by. Drivers waiting in their cars drummed on their steering-wheels in irritation, or used their car phones, or simply sat and waited. Eventually the procession moved out of sight and with it went my excuse for sitting doing nothing.

I rang the Derbyshire number again. Still no reply. Then I rang the Berkerly Agency hoping I could work at Pinetrees that night.

I could almost hear Pauline shaking her head. 'Pinetrees is well staffed, Kate. Being private they always seem to have more than their fair share. I'll do my best, though; just occasionally they need a trained nurse to do some "specialling".'

'Well if anything does come up I'd be most grateful. I'll even do domestic work if necessary.' I sensed she suppressed a laugh as the phone went down.

The morning passed slowly. I debated with myself for some time about ringing Paul Oakby and decided that it wouldn't achieve anything. The person I had to find was Colin Tiffield.

Thankfully at lunchtime Hubert reappeared. I was so pleased to have someone to talk to that I forgave him his crack about my detecting skills. He was wearing his usual black pinstripe and he looked well pleased with himself.

'That,' he said, 'was some funeral. Really tasteful. The mourners thought it was a lovely send-off.'

'Who was the lucky recipient?' I asked. Usually I don't want to know but this funeral had obviously been rather special.

'The Longborough rag and bone man—Arnie Shorter. Great character. We'll never see his like again. He had two sons, neither following in his footsteps: one's an accountant, the other's an estate agent. Makes you think, doesn't it?'

'It certainly does, Hubert. I can remember the time when being an estate agent was more respectable than being a rag and bone man.'

A smile flicked across Hubert's mouth as quick as a tic and then he said good-naturedly, 'Just for that, Kate, you can buy me a pint at the Swan.'

'Well, I would buy you a pint but it doesn't seem right for me to be out enjoying myself with my only client holed up inside her house expecting a madman to put in an appearance at any moment.'

'Try not to enjoy it then,' Hubert responded, and I gave in.

The Swan boasted only four customers and a very gloomy landlord. One customer was complaining bitterly about the latest increase in the price of beer and the others agreed.

'It's not surprising our lads who go abroad are known as lager louts, is it? Can't bloody well afford to drink in this country, can they?'

'You're right, mate,' joined in a thick-set man in denims. 'I think it's a plot, a government plot to stop us going out at all. All us workers are expected to do is work and the poor buggers who've got no work are supposed to stay home watching the box.'

The previous speaker gave a loud 'Huh!' and thumped his glass back on the table. '*If* they've got a home. If it hasn't been repossessed by the grasping building societies.'

Hubert ushered me away from the bar at this point.

'I'll order you chicken and chips,' he said. Then he added, 'And a cider.'

I was about to disagree—I would have preferred a brandy—but then I realised that I still had the rest of the day to work and I needed a clear head to decide exactly my plan of action.

The pub landlord himself brought our food over to us. He was still very gloomy. Hubert had chosen home-made steak and kidney pie; it didn't look very home-made to me but I thought the accompanying carrots looked hand-chopped. Why is it, I wondered, that something and chips is never quite so disappointing as other meals. And, as much as chips are vilified in the press, at least no one gets food poisoning from them.

We didn't talk much until we'd almost finished our meal and then Hubert launched into his plans for funeral modernisation and one-upmanship over the Co-op.

'We could have a catering suite and a florist on site,' he mused, 'we could offer a complete package.'

'I'm sure you're right, Hubert,' I agreed. 'You do have to be competitive. It's like my job—if anything happens to Vanessa the whole of Longborough will find out and I'll be hard pressed to attract other clients.'

'Not necessarily,' said Hubert. 'They'd have to put up with you, wouldn't they? You've got no competition at all.'

'Thanks, Hubert. You fill me with optimism.' I finished my cider. 'I'll get you that pint I promised you now,' I said, standing up and putting my hand out for his glass.

'Oh no, you don't,' he said. 'I don't like to see women getting drinks at the bar.'

He walked off just as my mouth dropped open in surprise. When he came back with the drinks and continued with his funeral updating chat I guessed buying me lunch and drinks made him feel justified in monopolising the conversation.

During a lull as he supped his beer I said, 'I get the impression, Hubert, you don't want to talk about my one and only client.'

He looked at me steadily for a moment and then glanced towards the bar as though expecting a sudden influx of eavesdroppers.

'You surprise me at times, Kate. I mean you're a woman of the world and yet it doesn't seem to have crossed your mind, as it did mine at the funeral, that—'

'That what?'

'That the most obvious person to have murdered Mrs Brigstock was the person who was supposed to have found the body.'

'That's ridiculous,' I snapped. 'She couldn't possibly... I mean the writing on the mirror... she was in shock...' I tailed off, trying to think clearly. Hubert didn't reply and after a few moments I said, 'She's far too nice to murder anyone, especially one of her own patients. And why employ me?'

'Perhaps she thought you wouldn't come up with anything.'

'Meaning I'm not a very good investigator. I'm learning all the time and, believe me, if there was a course in detective work I'd take it—'

'Now then, Kate,' interrupted Hubert. 'I didn't mean to upset you. I was only suggesting that perhaps your client is, well... madder than you think.'

I was silent for a moment. Vanessa was worried, slightly depressed and who wouldn't be, but she wasn't mad, of that I was quite sure.

'How do you explain my being followed?'

'Followed?' queried Hubert, his eyebrows raised in surprise.

'Yes. I told you about it.'

Hubert shook his head. 'You didn't,' he said.

'I'm sure I did,' I mumbled, half to myself and not sure at all.

'Did you actually see his face? Could you describe him?'

'Well, no... but I knew he was there.'

'How?'

'Stop it, Hubert, you're confusing me. I know I was being followed. I could feel he was there.'

Hubert held his head questioningly on one side. 'The power of suggestion can be very strong. Vanessa tells you she is being followed and after a while you begin to look over your shoulder too.'

'I'm not that susceptible and you've forgotten one thing.' I paused then for maximum effect. Hubert was trying to undermine my confidence or so I thought. 'I have heard his voice on the phone. He made threats...'

'He did what?' asked Hubert with one of his exasperated 'Why am I always kept in the dark' frowns. 'What exactly did he say?'

'It wasn't really what he said, Hubert, it was the fact he knew who I was and where I lived.'

Hubert wasn't to be fobbed off with that. 'Come on, Kate. What threats did he make?'

'Oh, all right, if you must know he said I'd better get a slab ready for myself.'

Hubert's small mouth tightened into pencil-line thinness and he stared into space for a moment. Then he said thoughtfully, 'She could have paid someone to make that call, you know. To convince you that a man does exist...'

'A man does exist. She's named him and I shall find him.'

'As I see it,' said Hubert slowly, 'there might well be a man but how do we know he means Vanessa any harm? He's made threats against you. Has he made any threats against her?'

Well had he? I tried hard to remember what Vanessa had said were his exact words. He'd professed love, I remembered that and he'd promised they would be together soon. And he'd said, 'I'm always watching you.' Did that mean literally? I wondered. Was he poised somewhere with a pair of binoculars? Across the road

perhaps, or at the back. There were alleyways at the back
of the houses in Percival Road . . .

'Another drink?' Hubert was saying.

I nodded.

As he went to the bar I imagined the bar as it had been
before the recession really took hold. Groups of men
holding forth on the economy, on sport, on their plans
for expansion. Respectable men, men from offices and
banks, men with emotional problems, sexual problems,
lonely men . . . men who might be obsessed with the pretty
district nurse they saw often in Longborough. Did they
have a penchant for uniform? Or was it just nurses they
liked? Or just the one nurse? Or? And then the thought
struck me . . . I had been thinking about men, not man.
Men in the plural. Perhaps there was more than one.

TWELVE

ON MY WAY back to the office Hubert asked me what my plans were for the afternoon.

'I'm not sure,' I answered. 'Make a list, drink coffee and try that Derbyshire number again. Then if I can psych myself up for it I shall pay visits to a couple of Vanessa's ex-boyfriends and finally I shall go round to Percival Road and surveille number thirty-six. Will I be earning my money doing that, Hubert?'

Hubert nodded. 'I was just thinking,' he said, 'if you weren't that busy perhaps you could help me.'

'Doing what?' I asked, mildly horrified.

'Just driving,' said Hubert. 'One of the Daimlers. A driver's gone off sick.'

'No, definitely no,' I said. 'Next you'll be asking me to do a bit of pall-bearing dressed as a man.'

Hubert tried not to smile and I realised why he'd been so keen to buy me lunch. He asked me one more time but I was adamant.

'I'll do it myself then,' he said.

'You do that, Hubert.'

He left me at the side entrance muttering, 'Just you wait till you want some help.'

In my office I made coffee straight away, organised myself with paper and pen and wrote a list of impending jobs. Once I'd done that I felt quite self-righteous. First on the list was ringing my client's sister. There was no reply, but I did have the satisfaction of ticking off number one on my list. Numbers two, three and four were the three men I knew who lived in or around Longborough: Ray Potten, Andrew Norten; and Paul Oakby, I thought, deserved one more meeting.

I made three calls. Andrew Norten's phone went un- answered, Paul Oakby was on patrol and I left a polite request with the desk Sergeant for him to ring me as soon as possible. Then I struck lucky: Ray Potten was in.

Feeling pleased that I could at least begin some sort of elimination process I drove to Station Lane to find Ray Potten.

Station Lane was well named: it was near a station but only a derelict one. The houses nearby had obviously been built for the rail workers; now they were overgrown with weeds, some had boarded-up windows and al- though I'd never seen a squatters' paradise, this was surely it. Number two looked both uninhabited and un- inhabitable. The front door had rotted at the hinges, the window-sills had fist-sized holes and the brickwork needed not so much repointing, as replacing.

When Ray Potten answered the door and asked me in it was not merely a question of opening the door; he had to lift the door with both hands. A naked light bulb lit the dark hall and in that light his sallow complexion seemed almost mask-like. He wore his straight dark hair in a pony-tail and he was dressed in black paint-spattered jeans and a plain black sweatshirt holed in places. Dan- gling from his right ear was a silver skull. I guessed he was about forty.

'It's warped with age like me, dear,' he said in a high, playfully camp voice as he lifted and then managed to push the door shut. 'Come on through to the studio.'

The 'studio' was the front room and just about every- thing an artist could need was crammed in there. The table, covered with newspaper, was home to a metal structure that resembled a four-legged insect with three antennae.

'I call that the state of the world,' he said, 'but you can call it what you like.'

Propped against the walls were various canvases, mostly depicting nightmarish scenes of the Vietnam War. As I stared at them he said, 'Have you any idea of the hell of the Vietnam War? Look at my sculpture.'

I looked at the 'insect'.

'See, see. That's what Agent Orange did—mutation. That's what all wars do. Mutate us. War diminishes us all. Do we care, though? Do we hell!'

'I haven't got much time, Mr Potten. I did explain I wanted just a few minutes with you to talk about Vanessa Wootten.'

'Sit down, dear. Do sit down.'

I looked around for a chair. There wasn't one.

'On the floor. Kate, isn't it?'

I nodded and found a space on a sheet of newspaper that seemed marginally cleaner than bare floorboards. He sat beside me but I got the impression sitting down wasn't something he did much of.

'Fire away then, Kate,' he said once we were both cross-legged on the floor. 'What little gems can I offer about feminine psychology?'

'I believe you knew Vanessa and did in fact go out with her for a few months.'

'That is correct. Only we didn't go out often. Vanessa liked to come here to chat.'

'Was she interested in art?' I asked.

Ray Potten smiled sardonically. 'You don't think she could have been interested in my body, then.'

'I didn't say that.'

'No, dear, you didn't have to,' he said, showing me a limp wrist.

'You're gay?' I said, which seemed stupidly obvious.

'No. Actually I'm straight, I'm just very good at pretending and I do have a lot of gay friends. It rubs off and I like to shock people. Also, there is a prejudice that somehow homosexuals are more artistic, more sensitive. It's good for business anyway.'

'I see. So you did have a sexual relationship with Vanessa.'

'No, I didn't say that. Vanessa thought I was gay too. And as I liked her very much, I let her go on thinking so. I told you just now that I was straight, but to be strictly accurate I suppose I'm really just a neutral. A nothing, no real sex drive at all.'

He fell silent for a moment, as if this revelation had cost him dear. Then he continued, 'We met at a small exhibition I had at the public library. I fell a little in love then, she's so beautiful. And her eyes so childlike but without the innocence, so haunted. I wanted to capture them on canvas. She's like a war victim herself; there's a lot of suffering in those eyes.'

'And did you capture them?'

'Yes, certainly. Once I'd finished the picture she never came here again. That was the end. I don't think she liked what she saw.'

'May I see it?'

'You may.'

From behind a pile of canvases he found a small framed picture.

'I keep it hidden. I don't plan to sell it,' he said as he handed it to me.

I held the picture at arm's length. It was of an oval face shape on a greenish background. A thin red line depicted a slit for a mouth. The only other feature was one blue eye, bloody and gouged out, hanging by a stalk.

Shuddering, I quickly handed it back to him. 'I'm not surprised she didn't come back,' I said. 'It's horrific.'

'Yes,' he said. 'It shows how blind she is. Poor Vanessa. She cannot verbalise her problems, you see. Can't share. I tried to get her to talk about her childhood but she wouldn't have it. Once she said, "My childhood was wiped away, it never existed." I thought as she couldn't talk about it I'd encourage her to paint. She just painted the one, finished before I painted the one of her. Would you like to see it?'

While Ray was upstairs I thought about the old saying of a picture being worth a thousand words. And hoped it was true. When he came down carrying a framed canvas he was also smoking. I recognised the smell and it wasn't tobacco.

'I think it's quite good,' he said. 'Stark in its simplicity but striking.'

He held it up a few feet from me. It was of a mirror. Reflected in the glass was a golden-headed child and behind her, tall and menacing, two headless black shapes.

'Who are they?' I asked.

Ray shook his head. 'I asked the same question of course. She clammed up. I've studied it long and hard since. One of the figures is female, I think, but other than that, no clues.'

'Did Vanessa ever mention being followed?'

'Often,' Ray answered with a shrug. 'She believed she was being pursued, of course, and I did warn her about crying wolf.'

'You didn't believe her, then.'

'I didn't say that, Kate. It was her reality not mine. I never actually saw anyone but she saw him, just as surely as she sees those shapes in the mirror.'

'Did you ever try to get in contact with Vanessa again?'

Ray Potten stared at me for a moment. Then he said, 'She'll come back when she's ready. She likes me, she'd like to be as unconventional as me. When you sort out her problems she'll be back.'

That seemed like an unfair burden to place on me but I smiled and said, 'I'll do my best.'

It was time to leave but I had one last question. 'Ray, what sort of car do you own?'

He laughed. 'Well, bless you, dear, for thinking I'm talented enough to be able to afford one. Wouldn't do me much good anyway.'

'Why's that?'

'Simple. I can't drive.'

As I left Station Lane I glanced at my watch. It was nearly four. I decided to spend some time outside Vanessa's house.

I parked a little way from number thirty-six Percival Road. I wasn't prepared for a long stay. One bar of chocolate and a half packet of Polos wouldn't keep me going for long. I sucked the mints slowly and watched as the residents came home from work. Very soon daylight began to fade and lights went on and curtains were drawn. And I suddenly felt so lonely I could have cried.

Just keep your mind on the job, I told myself; it's no use getting maudlin because it's dusk and your mother's in Australia and there's no man in your life. And that thought cheered me up. Because I did have a man of sorts and he was no bother: he was safe, reliable, bought me chips and didn't expect anything of me. So far he hadn't even put up my rent. And quite often he made me laugh.

My reverie was interrupted by the arrival of a car that parked outside thirty-six. I knew immediately who it was. He sat for a short time in his car and then slowly got out and walked to the front door of thirty-six. Both upstairs and downstairs lights were on but at first there was no response to Christopher Collicot's brisk knocking. Then I saw Vanessa peer from behind a curtain downstairs and moments later she opened the door slightly so that I could see just the side of her face until, that is, Christopher moved in front of her.

I couldn't hear what was being said but from Christopher's body language it looked as if he'd been invited in and had refused. Today he wore a white baseball cap, some sort of bomber jacket and jeans. The conversation was short, but judging by Christopher's wave and the quickness of his steps back to the car he seemed more cheerful and confident. I watched as he drove away and decided that I would be her next visitor.

I waited until six o'clock. That meant I'd done more than two hours of solid surveillance and I felt that was long enough. My feet were numb, my hands were cold and I was thirsty. Inside was warmth and with any luck hot coffee.

Vanessa answered my knocking quickly. I heard her run down the stairs and rush along the hall. It was as she threw open the door I realised why—she was expecting someone else. She was expecting a man, that was obvious. She wore a black shiny blouse with blue silk culottes, a double gold chain round her neck and those hoops of gold dangled from her ears. Her hair seemed softer and more fluffy and her eyes sparkled. At least they did until she saw me.

'Oh, it's you,' she said.

'May I come in?'

'Yes, of course, Kate, I'm sorry. It's just that I'm expecting someone. Come on through, I'll make you some
coffee—you look perished.'

She ushered me to the kitchen and began making real
coffee. I sat at the table and watched her.

'You're looking much better,' I said.

'I'm feeling much better, I feel great. I'm even going
back to work next week.'

I looked at her warily. Was she manic? I wondered. She
seemed suddenly cheerful given the circumstances. But
would a psychiatrist call it the manic phase of a paranoid manic depressive or was she merely on a high?

'Will you be able to cope with work?' I asked.

She smiled. 'Frederic is going to let someone accom-
pany me on my rounds.'

'Has he anyone in mind?'

'Yes, you, Kate!'

I laughed. 'I expect I'm the cheaper option.'

As Vanessa handed me a cup of coffee I told her I'd
had no joy with her sister's number. I noticed she trembled slightly as she sat down.

'But I have met Ray Potten,' I said. 'Seems a nice
enough person and fond of you. He thinks you'll re-
sume your relationship with him.'

Vanessa smiled in a non-committal way. 'I was fond of
him too. He wanted to sort me out, though, to talk about
my past. I don't want to rake things up. I want to live for
now and the future, not in the past.'

'But will your past let you do that?' I asked.

'Please, Kate, I know I haven't told you much but you
will find out in the end, I know you will. And I have told
you who I think he is. If you knew how hard I try to keep
myself on an even keel you'd understand. Sometimes,
just sometimes, I can forget he's out there. But that's

usually when I'm with another man. Someone who will protect me. That's why I went out with Paul Oakby. He was big and strong, I thought, and he was a policeman.'

'But then you said he raped you.'

Vanessa slumped forward slightly on the table and cradled her face in her hands. 'I've spoken about that to my psychiatrist. He suggests I try hypnosis. He seems to think that I may have been...mistaken. He says I have severe sexual problems and until they are sorted out I shouldn't have any more serious relationships.'

'I see,' I said, but I wasn't sure that I did. I finished my coffee and asked casually, 'Was there any special reason that Christopher Collicot called this evening?'

She smiled. 'Oh, he's sweet. He only called to see how I was and to ask if I was up to helping out with Farley Wood's spring fête cum jumble sale. I said I'd think about it.'

As I stood up to go I said, 'One last question, Vanessa, something that's puzzling me...'

'Yes?'

'Exactly how long have you suspected you are being followed?'

She paused and paled a little. 'Three years,' she said after a long pause. 'Not all the time of course. But on and off. So that sometimes I've doubted my own sanity. Now he's closing in on me, isn't he? Coming in for the kill.'

'You mean Colin Tiffield?'

'Yes,' she said firmly.

Vanessa was silent as she led me through to the hall. I was just about to say good-bye when there was a knock at the door. We were both startled and Vanessa's earrings swung a little and sparkled and just for a moment I stood mesmerised. Then the knocking became more insistent and she abruptly opened the door.

It was Frederic Tissot. They didn't have to say anything for me to realise that they were, or had just become, more than colleagues. The eye contact was sustained just a fraction too long.

'I'll ring you,' I called out as I left, but there was no reply.

So much for the happy family photograph.

THIRTEEN

As I WALKED to the car I tried to work out why I hadn't guessed about their relationship. I decided I wasn't being particularly dimwitted. That I had been right to be a tinge suspicious of any man who keeps a photo of his wife and child on display and that judging by Vanessa's mood, the carefully chosen clothes and the glow of fresh make-up, Frederic was still in the embryonic lover stage. And therefore not a suspect in pathological pursuing games.

Hubert was in his flat upstairs when I arrived back at Humberstones. His curtains were drawn but a friendly glow surrounded the top half of the building. It was as I drove round to the parking area that I saw the police car. By the time I'd switched off the ignition and momentarily listened with disgust as the engine ran on, Paul Oakby was opening my car door. This was the first time I had seen him in uniform and it improved him. Somehow he seemed less menacing; no doubt in a crisis he could have even looked quite reassuring.

'You left a message, Miss Kinsella,' he said coldly.

'I did indeed, Officer. Thanks for coming. You were lucky to find me.'

'I saw your car outside Vanessa's place. I thought you'd be back.'

'You'd better come up to the office.'

He smirked at me like a naughty schoolboy but the smirk didn't last. The experience of being in an undertaker's seemed to have a chastening effect.

'How do you stick working here?' he asked as he followed me up the stairs.

'I'm warped,' I said, turning in the half light and smiling so that he knew I was in no way worried by his presence.

He raised an eyebrow as if to say that could explain it.

Once in my office he sat down, without being asked, in a sprawl of heavy uniformed masculinity on one of my office swivel chairs. 'Now then,' he began, as if it was his office and not mine, 'what's this all about? I thought we'd had our little chat and that was the end of it. Found you couldn't resist me, eh?'

I didn't rise to the bait but I did want a little nibble. 'Thank you for coming,' I said, trying to sound gracious. 'I'd like to ask you a couple more questions.'

'I'm listening.'

'Vanessa tells me you were . . . a bit jealous at times.'

'I wouldn't deny that.'

'And did that jealousy make you think Vanessa was two-timing you?'

'Of course she was.'

'And what did you do about it?'

'Well, as I told you before, I didn't rape her. And I wasn't about to lose any sleep over the wallies she knows.'

Momentarily I stared into his cold blue eyes. 'Do you still have your key to Vanessa's house?'

He nodded, still staring.

'I'd like it back.'

'I'll deliver it to her personally,' he said.

'No, don't do that she's . . .'

'She's what?'

'She's been burgled—'

I didn't get a chance to finish. Paul Oakby suddenly got very angry, his face turned a nasty puce colour and his fist banged down on my desk as if I was personally responsible.

'When did this happen? She hasn't reported it, you know. The stupid cow. Are you *sure* you know what you're doing?'

'Constable Oakby, do *you* want to help Vanessa?'

The tone of my voice seemed to calm him. 'Yeah, yeah. What the hell is going on, though?'

'I wish I knew. But now I do have a name.'

'Who?'

'If I tell you will you promise to...' I paused. What on earth did I want him to do? 'Would you be willing to help me? Through the proper channels, of course.'

'What's the bastard's name?'

'At the moment that is all I do have, just the name. But I think he may have a criminal record. Vanessa thinks he's evil and she's convinced it's him. And so far I haven't got any other real suspects.'

Paul Oakby's colour still remained high and I hoped I was doing the right thing in even telling him about the burglary. For some reason I felt that he might prove useful. He was after all physically strong and although perhaps not CID material he was on the inside.

'The only thing stolen from her house,' I continued, 'was her work diary and that means that if she goes back to work he'll know exactly where she is at any time of the day. Vanessa seems to think her sister may know where this man is but if you could trace his present address and check to see if he has a criminal record.'

'It's as good as done,' he said grimly. 'I'll find out about the bastard.'

'Let me know, won't you? And be discreet, because if CID find out you've been ... unprofessional—the force might use it as an excuse to get rid of you.'

He was silent for a moment. 'I never was flavour of the month but I'm no hero. Anyway Vanessa and me are finished. I'll do this for old times' sake. Now what's his name?'

I told him and he repeated it quietly, as if to himself.

'As soon as I find out anything I'll be in touch,' he said as he stood up to go.

I heard him walk down the stairs and close the side door with a bang. And then the worry began. What had I done? If he did find out where Colin Tiffield lived would he go charging off flinging punches and accusations at a man who might be completely innocent of harassment and murder?

I was sitting, head in hands, when Hubert walked in.

'Who was that just leaving?' he asked. 'And what's wrong with you?'

After a fairly long explanation he tutted a bit. 'Well, there is only one thing you can do,' he said.

'What's that?'

'Pray.'

'That's very helpful, Hubert, thank you.'

I must have looked miserable because he then said, 'Cheer up, Kate. With any luck he won't find out anything and perhaps you can get to this Colin Tiffield first.'

'Maybe,' I said, 'but I'm beginning to think that I should give up trying to be a detective. I'm just not suited to it. I shouldn't have been swayed by the sight of him in uniform. It made him seem somehow more solid and reliable.'

Hubert didn't quite know what to say to that so I picked up the phone and dialled the Derbyshire number again. There was still no reply. Just as I'd replaced the receiver it began ringing. Startled, I snatched up the handset.

'That was quick,' said Pauline Berkerly. 'Were you expecting a call?'

'No, Pauline, just reflexes honed by constant use.'

'I'm glad I've got hold of you. I rang your home number just now and thought I might as well have a stab at your office. You remember you were looking for work at Pinetrees? Well, there's one night's specialling going.'

'Great. When?'

'Ah! There lies the thorn in the rose. It's tonight.'

She didn't give me a chance to reply and I felt my spirits sag even further. I was exhausted. All I wanted to do was sink a cocoa with brandy, fill a hot-water bottle and escape into sleep.

'I know it's short notice,' Pauline was saying, 'but someone has just rung in sick and I can't find a replacement at such short notice. Please say yes, Kate, I'm really desperate. You'll save my business reputation.'

'All right Pauline,' I said, reluctantly waving good-bye to both bed and cocoa. 'Because it's you I will, but if I get the sack because I fall asleep your reputation will still suffer.'

'You won't let me down, Kate. Thanks. You never know, it could be a useful night's work. Could you be there by ten?' Then before I could say anything she added, 'By the way, you'll be looking after a young doctor who's alcoholic and suicidal, but I don't think he'll give you any trouble.'

I didn't speak for a moment. It sounded like hard work sitting for hours by the bedside of some poor demented medic.

'Kate, are you still there?'

I looked at my watch; it was seven thirty. 'I'll be there,' I said.

Hubert seemed surprised when I told him I was going to work that night.

'You'll be very tired,' he said.

'There's no need to state the obvious,' I snapped.

Hubert squinted at me. 'You're not usually in such a bad mood,' he observed. 'You must be hungry.'

I scowled.

'I'll go out for fish and chips if you like.'

'Chips twice in one day is pushing it a bit.'

'In that case I could get Chinese.'

I shrugged. 'Only if *you* want it, Hubert. Don't bother about any for me.'

'I won't then,' he said.

When he'd gone I washed my hair in the sink, had a quick scrub down and put on a dark blue uniform dress. It matched my mood. Now that Hubert had suggested I might be hungry I realised I was and I hoped that he didn't plan to eat his sweet and sour pork, special fried rice and chicken and cashew nuts in front of me.

A few minutes later I heard him come up the stairs. He paused for a second by my door and then walked straight on past. Well that just serves you right, I thought. You've upset Hubert and now you've missed out on a Chinese meal. I looked in my office drawer for a snack and found a few cream crackers and an overripe banana. That would have to do.

I'd just put them on a paper towel when Hubert walked in. He couldn't knock first, he had his hands full with two bags of Chinese food, plates, napkins and cutlery.

'Well you could have cleared the desk,' he said.

I hurried to remove various bits of paper debris and soon Hubert had set a feast before me.

'I didn't bring chopsticks,' he said. 'I thought you might skewer me through the heart.'

'Hubert,' I said, 'how would I manage without you?'

His mouth puckered into a smile and then he said, 'Come on, Kate, for goodness' sake eat it before it gets cold. It cost me a fortune.'

THE NARROW LANE that led to Pinetrees Psychiatric Hospital was lit only by a wrought-iron lamp standard at its entrance. My main beam lit the long dark path ahead, gathering in the gloom of naked branches and bushes that clawed together in a sinister bower. Eventually the lane widened and I could see the hospital in all its grandeur. Pine trees did indeed encircle the building and as I neared it I could see chandeliers hanging as brightly as Christmas decorations. There were two more lamp standards either end of the building so that the rolling lawns in front were highlighted in all their clipped elegance.

I parked my car directly outside the front entrance. Pinetrees was a vast mansion, so well lit that inside I could see dark panelled wood and thick curtains and almost smell the opulence of a bygone era. On my right, in a corner of the grounds, I could see a small church whose lights were reflected through stained-glass windows, shedding patterns of red and gold on the grass in front.

Inside, behind an alcove of wood panelling, sat a uniformed man. He was dressed like a hotel commissionaire—all blue serge and brass buttons. He called me 'love' and took me partway along a corridor to a door with a black plaque lettered in gold—THE CHURCHILL SUITE.

'In there, love. The charge nurse will meet you.'

I became aware then of the low throb of pop music coming from behind the door. I knocked and waited for a moment, then I turned the old-fashioned china handle.

It was a large room, wood-panelled with high ceilings, ornate cornices and with two sparkling chandeliers that would have looked at home in a ballroom. By the grand piano a string orchestra should have been in position playing Strauss waltzes while ladies in long frocks fanned themselves and waited for their dance partners to fulfil their obligations. Instead, the piano sat as mute as the twenty or so people sitting on high-backed chairs with round tables in front of them. Some had turned to look at me but then with the resigned look of professional patients they returned to their glasses of Coke or orange juice and to conversations with themselves or with their table companions. A few continued to stare into space.

A short, balding man in jeans and a check shirt seemed to be trying to encourage a couple to dance but on seeing me he waved and called out, 'Won't be a moment.' And then with a final word to the couple he beckoned me to join him.

'Saturday night dance,' he said by way of explanation as I approached.

I smiled sympathetically. I knew just how gruelling the Saturday night dance could be, although I had to admit NHS mental hospital dances were nothing like this.

'I'm Kate Kinsella from the Berkerly.'

'Oh, yes. You're for young Dr Guilsborough. I'll get one of the residents to show you to his floor.'

He called 'Alan' to a man sitting alone at one of the tables and Alan promptly stood up and walked over to us.

'Take Miss Kinsella to Nightingale floor, will you. To the nurse in charge.'

Alan was, I supposed, in his twenties, tall and very thin, with thick black unruly hair. His trousers ended well above his ankles and from his jacket sleeves thin hairy wrists emerged, attached to hands that seemed to swing independently. One of these he shook towards the door, saying in a low monotone, 'Come on. Come on. Come on.'

I followed him past more wood panelling, up a wide staircase, along yet another corridor to the nurses' office. The nurse in charge wore no uniform, just a chunky blue sweater and a navy skirt and a badge with her name and 'Staff Nurse' underneath. Alan left me without comment.

'You wouldn't think he used to be a pop star, would you?' she said as we watched him shuffling back along the corridor. 'You're the special?'

I nodded.

She flicked over the Kardex and began reading. Young and pretty, she obviously didn't want to be late off duty.

'"Dr Jonathan Guilsborough, aged twenty-eight,"'she began. '"Admitted this morning following a suicide attempt, tried to throw himself from a bridge. Saved by a passer-by. Seen by the consultant psychiatrist on admission. All routine observations normal. Parents have reported steady deterioration over past few months. Appetite poor, alcohol consumption high, declining standards of dress and hygiene. Responding well to staff. Talkative at times. Appears co-operative. To be observed at all times. Anti-depressants commenced. For review in the near future. Query—to commence ECT.'"

'Any questions?' she asked, smiling, but it was clear she neither wanted nor expected any.

I shook my head.

'He's been given a bath,' she said.

'Oh good.'

'I'll take you to his room. One of the night staff will relieve you for meals.'

I followed her to a room two doors from the office.

'Be a dear and introduce yourself. I've got a date and you know how it is.'

I smiled as if I did, but my last date had been so long ago that I had in fact forgotten.

Dr Guilsborough lay on the bed fully dressed. On a chair by his side a middle-aged woman with grey wavy hair and round shoulders sat knitting.

'Oh good. You the special?' she asked.

I nodded. 'I'm Kate.'

'Had the report?' she asked, eyes down, finishing the last few stitches on her needles.

'Yes, thanks.'

'Good. I'll be off then,' she said, placing her knitting in a shopping bag. 'I've been on twelve hours. I've had enough.' As she opened the door she said cheerfully, 'See you tomorrow then, Jonathan. Be good.'

Jonathan didn't answer. Instead his eyes roved up and down my body and he smiled a vague dreamy kind of smile as if he'd just found gold top instead of skimmed milk.

'Hello, Dr Guilsborough,' I said. 'I'm Kate Kinsella.'

'Call me Jonathan,' he said.

The room, though spacious, contained only the bed covered with a padded cream bedspread, one armchair, a bedside table, a gold fringed lamp and a TV on a trolley in a corner of the room. There was a walk-in cupboard and a door which I presumed led to the en-suite shower and loo. And all round the room the walls were covered with the ubiquitous dark oak wood panelling.

'There's no escape,' he said, standing up and signalling for me to sit down.

This wasn't what I had imagined. I'd expected him to be in a poor state physically as well as mentally. Instead

he looked young, fresh and eager. His complexion was
pallid, his eyes hazel, his lips red and full. I supposed he
was an average sort of build and height but thick black
curly hair added a couple of inches to his height.

'This is cosy,' he said with the same vague smile. 'Are
you single?'

'I am.'

'Good. It's going to be a long night.'

And he smiled again.

FOURTEEN

A WHOLE NIGHT! Eleven hours! I had no knitting with me, because I'd never learned how; I was halfway through a paperback book, but if the other half was as dull as the first I'd have real trouble staying awake.

'Relax, Kate. I'm not going to give you any problems,' said Jonathan as he sat on the bed and stared at me. 'On the other hand I'm not going to sleep either.'

'I'm glad you're not going to give me any problems, but why no sleep?'

He shrugged. 'Let's just say I wouldn't want to miss any time with an attractive young redhead.'

I didn't quite know how to answer that so I smiled, deciding that like mad dogs, mad medics could probably smell fear. I pushed from my mind all the things that could happen. Instead, I tried to concentrate my thoughts on his fear, the fact that he was ill, that he needed a sympathetic ear.

'Is there anything you'd like to do, Jonathan—watch television, play cards, talk?'

'We could screw.'

'We could,' I said. 'But we're not going to.'

'All the girls I meet say that. What's wrong with me? Go on, tell me ... I can take it. Is it my looks? I never manage to keep my girlfriends for long. I'm not repulsive, am I?'

'Of course not. You're good-looking enough. Perhaps you just try to rush them.'

He thought about that for a while as he began to pace the floor and as he did so, he swept his hand through his hair over and over again as if that would somehow smooth out his thoughts. Eventually, as the pacing continued I realised he had forgotten the question and that I was there.

On the assumption that he would be more relaxed lying down I said, 'Why don't you get undressed and get into bed? We could talk properly then.'

'Right,' he said, his red lips forming a half smile that just missed being a leer. He began to remove his sweater and jeans. He let them fall into a pile at his feet and stood there in red and white spotted boxer shorts waiting for my reaction.

It was the bruises that surprised me. On both shins and upper arms vivid stains, like blue ink, mingled with red grazed patches and, as if to punish me for my reaction, he swiftly removed his underpants and stood naked before me.

'Seen all you want to?'

'Good body,' I said. 'Shame about the bruises. They must be painful.'

I tried to imagine the scenario of Jonathan trying to throw himself over the bridge and the brave passer-by who clung on to his legs and managed to haul him back again. It was no wonder he was bruised.

His bravado failed then, his eyes filling with tears, and I stood up and looked away, wishing I felt more able to cope. Wishing I wasn't there. Wishing I could do something.

When I looked back Jonathan was in bed, curled into the foetal position—sobbing.

I sat down, pulled the armchair close to the bed and patted his shoulder. After a while he stopped crying and became quiet and then he appeared to doze. I simply sat and watched him.

At ten thirty the door opened quietly and a woman carrying a torch beckoned me outside. She was, I supposed, in her thirties, pretty, wearing a dark grey suit and white blouse and with short brown hair that curved around her cheeks. A huge bunch of keys rattled noisily at her waist.

'I'm the night nursing manager. Is he asleep?' she whispered.

'I think so,' I whispered back. 'But he could be faking.'

'Keep a really close eye on him, Nurse. Don't leave him for an instant. He knows this hospital very well. Our Jonathan won't hesitate to take advantage of you.'

'You mean he's been in before?'

'Oh, yes. Didn't they tell you that during the report?'

I shook my head.

'This is his third suicide attempt and his fourth admission. We really know him quite well. Try to persuade him to take his medication, won't you?'

'Of course.'

'Press the bell on the wall if he gets difficult. Don't hesitate.'

I promised I wouldn't. 'Is he likely to be difficult?'

Smiling, she patted my arm. 'Don't look so worried. He's not likely to rape you but he can become very wearing, so do ring the bell if you want a break or to go to the loo.' She left after explaining the night sedation would be brought along shortly with hot drinks and biscuits and that at one o'clock I would be relieved for an hour's meal break.

I resumed my vigil by the bed and tried to read my book. I couldn't concentrate and at eleven I heard a clock chiming and somewhere in the building someone screamed.

Jonathan opened his eyes. 'Where's that bloody night nurse?' he asked, perching on one elbow and peering at me with a creased face and dull eyes.

'Do you want your night sedation? I could ring for it.'

'It's not the Ritz. She'll be along. It could be Sally. I like her. She's got big tits—bigger than yours.'

'That's not hard,' I said.

'Cool bitch,' he said unaggressively. 'Hold my hand.'

His hand felt cold. The fingers were long and thin.

'Did you do much surgery?' I asked.

'Think they are surgeon's hands, do you?'

'Could be.'

'Well, the only surgery I've done is a couple of appendicectomies, three hernias and several ingrowing toenails, and I made a hash of all of them.'

'You prefer medicine then?'

He laughed bitterly. 'I don't prefer anything. I'm not good at playing doctors. The only thing I like about being a doctor is that I get to meet a few nubile young nurses.'

'That's some compensation I suppose,' I said uneasily. 'You get turned on by nurses, do you? In uniform?'

'Yes. Anything wrong with that?'

'No, of course not. If all you do is look.'

'What's that supposed to mean?'

Before I had time to answer there was a knock at the door and a young woman, blonde hair in a pony-tail and breasts crammed into a pink blouse, walked in with a tray. I assumed this was Sally. She smiled at me in a friendly way and walked over to the bed.

'Hi, Jonathan. There was no need to go to such lengths to see me again, you know. You could have come back as a voluntary patient.'

He smiled at her languidly. 'You know I'm in love with you. I can't resist your... charms.'

'Seriously, Jonathan, last time you were in here you made really good progress. You'd even found a job, hadn't you?'

He nodded and as he did so grabbed her hand and pulled her nearer to the bed.

'I've got work to do,' she said, extricating his long fingers and firmly placing his hand back on the bed.

'Come back later then,' he said. 'Kate won't mind, will you.'

'Not at all,' I said.

Sally smiled, showing a neat row of white teeth. 'I'll be back at one to relieve Kate for her meal break.'

'Good, I'll take my night sedation then.'

Sally shrugged and smiled at me wearily as if this was the normal course of events and there wasn't much she could do about it. And then she left, leaving a faint wisp of some exotic perfume and somehow without her there the room seemed darker and more chill.

Jonathan lay back on the bed and stared at the ceiling and ignored me even when I offered him the mug of cocoa Sally had left. I returned to my book, drank my cocoa, ate two biscuits, and tried to make sense of the words and not think too much.

Eventually he spoke. 'I've made a real cock-up of my life.'

'In what way?' I asked as I looked up from my book.

'In every way I suppose. My parents wanted me to be a doctor. My older brother is an accountant, so I had to become a doctor.'

'Had to?'

'My mother pushed me. She wanted a doctor in the family. I was too weak to refuse. I don't even like the human race much, let alone feel motivated to save lives.'

'What would you rather have been?'

He paused and then said slowly, 'I wanted to be a pianist.'

'In a orchestra?'

'No. In a night-club.'

'You still could.'

'It's too late.'

I didn't disagree. He wanted to believe it was too late. Telling him he was young enough to start again wouldn't have helped. I stayed silent.

After a while he said, 'Tell me about you. Have you got a boyfriend?'

'Not at the moment. Perhaps I'm just too busy.'

'What doing?'

'Running a business. I provide a service—a sort of—' I struggled with the description. 'Well, I do research for people.'

'Such as?'

'At the moment I'm researching a friend of mine's family tree—Vanessa Wootten.'

His hand reached up and combed through his hair. Please don't know her, I thought. Please don't. But I knew by the slightly puzzled look on his face that he did.

'Nice little body,' he was saying. 'She was a patient here. I met her a few times. She was paranoid. Thought a man was following her. I chatted her up but she wasn't interested. Mind you, she was depressed.'

'Did she tell you who she thought was following her?'

'No. He wasn't anyone famous if that's what you mean. That's a fairly common feature, you know.

Thinking someone famous like Steve McQueen is communicating with you via the TV or film.'

'From beyond the grave in Steve's case,' I said, but he didn't seem to realise McQueen was dead and he looked at me blankly.

Then he said, 'There's a syndrome—De Clerambault's—where the sufferer believes that the loved one sends them coded messages.'

'You seem to know a lot about it.'

He smiled. 'I worked here for a while—before my breakdown.'

'And was that when you met Vanessa?'

'I was a patient when I met Vanessa otherwise I wouldn't have been chatting her up, would I?'

'And when was that?'

'Oh God, I can't remember. One, maybe two years ago. What does it matter? I thought we were talking about you anyway.'

'I was just curious, that's all. We're quite close at the moment. She lives in Longborough not far from me.'

'I live near Longborough—Upper Gaddington. When I get out of here we could meet. We could do a tour of all the pubs.'

'You have a car then?'

'Of course I've got a car. I've got two. Presents from adoring parents for passing my finals. They have plenty of money but as much sensitivity as gangrenous toes.'

'So you still live at home?'

'Yes, for Christ's sake. Not that abnormal, is it? I can't find a woman to live with me and I don't fancy living alone. You ask a lot of questions. I thought psychiatric nurses were meant to be good listeners not bloody interrogators.'

I apologised and suggested he got some sleep. 'No more questions,' I promised.

He closed his eyes then and after a while his breathing became deeper and a little later his eyes moved beneath their lids as though he was dreaming and I stretched my legs and sat back in the armchair. It was still only twelve and as the clock struck the hour I prayed he would sleep on and that I would be able to keep awake.

FIFTEEN

THE STAFF dining-room boasted harsh strip lighting and round pine tables with, at one end of the room, a buffet bar displaying cold meats and a variety of salads. The wood panelling shimmered a little in the bright light and made the six faces I could see appear shadowed and gaunt. Selecting a slice of unappetising pale meat and some coleslaw I then had to decide who to sit with. I chose a corner table where the two occupants, one male, one female, seemed chatty and cheerful.

'Hello, love,' said the middle-aged woman, who had a perm of frizzy silver grey curls and a pleasant smile. 'I haven't seen you before.'

'I'm agency,' I explained. 'Specialling.'

'Doc Guilsborough?'

I nodded as I sat down.

'Rather you than me, love. He can be dead depressing. Always sorry for himself, he is. I'm Lizzie and my handsome friend is Winston.'

Winston smiled. 'Hi there,' he said. His dark brown skin shone like the mahogany wood panelling and he gave the impression of good-natured strength. The sort of person who, when there was trouble, would stop potential riots with his mere presence. Not that he was particularly large, he just gave off confident vibes.

They chatted for a bit about the deteriorating food at night and then about the state of some of their patients and I listened and smiled and nodded.

During a lull I made my move as casually as I could: 'A friend of mine was in here once, Vanessa Wootten. She said the food was wonderful.'

There was no response at first, then Lizzie asked, 'Was she on Byron? A nurse, wasn't she?'

I nodded.

'Nurse and doctor patients never complain about the food. After all, they get treatment free here. It's the private patients who complain. Mind you, give me the aristos every day. It's the nouveau riche moaners who get up my nose.'

'I couldn't manage to visit her,' I explained. 'Was she all right when she left?'

Lizzie shrugged. 'She was less depressed but she was still telling the staff that a man wanted to get her. I think she was frustrated—just like poor Winston here.'

They both laughed uproariously at that, and I waited until they'd finished before saying, 'It couldn't have been true then? She's very attractive. I can understand someone having a crush on her.'

A look passed between them that I couldn't read and then Winston said, 'The doc quite fancied her but then he fancied everyone.'

And they laughed again at their own private joke and I realised I was on to a loser.

I finished my meal and excused myself.

'You can get coffee in the sitting-room,' said Lizzie, pointing to a door to my right.

I thanked her and entered a small bay-windowed room, empty of people but with faded chintzy armchairs, matching curtains, full ashtrays, empty cups and saucers and a smell of stale smoke.

I sat for a while and drank lukewarm coffee from a large Thermos jug, feeling lonely and out of things and

jealous of people everywhere who were tucked up warm
and safe in bed. Was Vanessa alone, I wondered, or still
with Frederic? Were they being watched while I merely
sat watching a man sleep? My night here hadn't gained
me any information about Vanessa but perhaps a few
door-to-door enquiries would help. That was what private investigators did—wasn't it? Sally seemed pleased to
see me on my return and although she didn't say anything she was obviously eager to go.

Jonathan appeared to be asleep. I stared for a while at
his back, then put my coat around me and tried to get
comfortable in the chair. My book wasn't improving and
the words kept moving in front of my eyes. I couldn't
help feeling resentful as I listened to his steady breathing. Each breath seemed like a lullaby and I found myself breathing at the same pace and that can lead to
falling asleep.

At four thirty I was thankful that Sally relieved me for
a half-hour's tea break but I was disappointed to have to
sit alone in the dining-room. I drank two cups of stewed
tea and ate bread and jam and pulled back the curtains
to stare out of the window on to the grounds. A tall clock
tower stood in the quadrangle outside, facing the bedrooms. Strange: I thought that in Victorian NHS psychiatric hospitals the clock always faced away from the
building as though telling the inmates that time no longer
mattered to them. Time mattered to me, though, and
when I heard the first chime of the hour I walked back to
the Nightingale suite, telling myself I only had three more
hours to keep myself awake.

Jonathan still lay in the same position and as I entered
the room Sally put a warning finger to her lips and whispered that I should let him sleep on in the morning, that
there was no point in waking him.

The three hours from then till eight stretched ahead about as invitingly as a long wait to see the dentist. Still, I consoled myself there was no pain at the end of it, just the blessed relief of sleep. And it was Sunday and I could sleep all day if I wanted to.

Jonathan slept on. I pulled the curtains, selfishly, just after seven so that I could see the daylight and watch the squirrels and see the day staff arrive for work. It was a bright clear morning and as Pinetrees began to wake up so did I. And I felt unnaturally cheerful. Night nurse's hysteria they call it. Mine was a mild case because real hysteria needs an audience and my patient slept on. We had both survived the night. And suddenly I was fired up with new enthusiasm for, well...everything. Hubert I would invite for a meal in the evening and tomorrow...tomorrow perhaps I'd have the case sorted. And after this successful case, there would be others, more prestigious, more lucrative. I could retire at forty to the south of France...

It was five to eight when Jonathan called me. I'd just put on my coat and picked up my bag.

'Kate.'

I stood by his bed as he turned sleepily to face me.

'Thanks for everything. Sorry I was such a nuisance.'

'That's all right. It was a pleasure.' And it was, now that it was over.

'About Vanessa?'

'Yes.'

'Get her to tell you about the rapes.'

'Don't you mean rape—singular?'

'No. Just ask her. She needs a friend.'

'But...I thought...'

Jonathan had turned and snuggled down again. That was all he was going to say on the subject and my new-found euphoria began slipping away from me like tallow flowing down the side of a candle—slow but constant.

By the time I had driven home the candle was down to a stub. I felt weary and defeated. I made a big bowl of porridge, added sugar and cream and ate it in bed. That cheered me slightly and as I drifted off to sleep I thought nothing could be better than a full stomach and a warm duvet and a long, long, sleep.

LOUD KNOCKING woke me. At first I stared at the alarm clock as if somehow it was responsible. Then I realised there was someone at the door. I pulled on a dressing-gown and walked slowly down the stairs. I still felt asleep. It was Mrs Morcott from the WI and Neighbourhood Watch.

'Having a lie in, dear? So sorry to disturb you on a Sunday morning. I've come to ask you a favour.'

I smiled weakly, sure that if I tried to speak no sound would come.

'It's about the fête and jumble sale on Tuesday after-noon. There's so much flu around that I've lost three helpers and I've got to find replacements. It starts at two and I'm sure it will be all finished by five. Could you be a dear and give us a hand?'

I nodded and smiled and managed to utter the word 'pleasure'. I wasn't sure it would be.

'Thank you so much, dear. I'll put you down for the ladies' clothes section. You'll be good at that. See you in the WI hall at about one-thirty.'

Back in bed I thought of all the stalls I could have served on: the cake stall, bric-à-brac, selling raffle tick-ets, making candy floss. Instead I'd got landed with the old clothes.

I'd woken up now but it was only twelve. I'll have one more try at Vanessa's sister, I thought. It would salve my conscience.

As I dialled the number from the phone in my front room I stared out at the triangle of grass, the bare oak tree and the graveyard beyond, and then as if to spoil my view and just as the number connected a dark green car drove past. At first I thought it was VMS, otherwise known as Christopher Collicot (poor thing), but the driver had a mass of dark hair so I must have been mistaken...

'Hello? Hello?' said a voice sharp with irritation.

Astonished that someone had replied I blurted out quickly, 'This is Kate Kinsella, you don't know me but...' I paused: when in doubt—lie. 'I'm your sister's social worker. I wondered if I might call on you. We have been having some problems and I thought perhaps you could cast some light on Vanessa's difficulties.'

There was a long pause, then she said, 'She's always caused problems, that girl. How long will it take?'

'Not long,' I assured her. 'An hour or so.'

'We're not on speaking terms. I don't know what she's been up to lately. And to be honest I don't really care. There are no children involved, I hope?'

'No. Nothing of that sort. I'd be most grateful.'

'Oh, all right then. There's no chance of a reconciliation so don't expect anything like that.'

'Thank you very much. Would this afternoon be convenient?'

'I suppose so. After three.'

'Fine. Thank you.'

'We're on top of the hill. You can't miss it.'

She sounded as if she hoped I would.

'Thank you again Mrs...'

'Miss—Sheila Wootten,' she supplied tersely.

Suddenly I was tired no longer. If I was to get to Derbyshire by three I would have to move myself. Then the phone rang. It was Hubert.

'Your voice sounds hoarse,' said Hubert.

'I'm off to Derbyshire today,' I said. 'I'm finally going to crack the case.'

Silence.

'Are you still there, Hubert?'

'Yes.'

'What's wrong?'

'What time will you be back?'

'Not late, why?'

'I wanted to invite you for a meal.'

'Great. A celebration?'

'My birthday.' He sounded miserable.

'Happy birthday to you, happy birthday to you,' I sang croakily until I was interrupted.

'That's enough of that,' said Hubert, 'you've got a voice like a drunken Irish navvy.'

'What time is the birthday meal?'

'Eight.'

'Fine. My voice will be in trim by then.'

'Take more than a few hours, that singing voice needs a transplanted larynx...'

'Just liquid lubrication that's all, Hubert.'

He didn't sound convinced but said he had plenty of wine to test out my theory.

I did wonder as I put down the phone why he should invite me. Until now he had managed to keep his flat upstairs as private as a holy of holies. Perhaps, of course, he had something to hide. Maybe he had a shoe collection that outshone Imelda Marcos's. Or perhaps he just valued his privacy.

Just before leaving I rang Vanessa. All seemed well, although when I mentioned the trip to Derbyshire her voice began to tremble.

'Do take care, Kate,' she said. 'You can't even trust my sister.'

SIXTEEN

DERBYSHIRE IN the rain and wind seemed wild and forlorn. The low stone walls separating empty fields seemed to stretch for miles but eventually I found the small village of Bonsall where I stopped a soaked local to ask directions to Maple Cottage.

''Bout a mile, uphill. Can't miss it,' he said, pointing me in the direction of a narrow winding road that did indeed go uphill.

It was nearly three but the light was poor and the sixty or so miles I'd driven was beginning to tell on me. The first sight of Maple Cottage made me feel even worse. It was large, stone-built but with mean small windows. The sort of windows that seem to spy on you. It was in total darkness and total solitude. Trees and bushes crowded around the sides of the house in what seemed like a planned attempt to increase privacy.

I parked the car on the muddy gravelled forecourt and walked quickly to the front porch that was straggled with ivy which hung just above my head like sinister claws. I knocked loudly, but I half hoped no one was at home. I'll knock one more time, I promised myself. Just once more. And then I heard footsteps coming down stairs and the click of a light switch and then the door opened.

'I was asleep,' said Sheila Wootten. 'Come in.'

Not having tried to look like a stereotypical social worker I was faintly disappointed that I had been so easily mistaken for one. Sheila Wootten, though, wasn't quite what I expected. She was at least twenty years older than her sister and although she shared the same blue-coloured eyes and fairish hair, there the similarity ended. She was tall and plump in a soft shapeless way, had several chins, and her hair had been backcombed in an attempt to cover its thinness. Her mouth was set in a downward line of discontent. She wore a loose beige Crimplene dress with a matching cardigan, enlivened, only slightly, by a large cameo brooch.

Inside, the cottage smelt damp, felt cold and, worst of all, gave off unfriendly vibes. I don't believe in ghosts but I do believe in atmosphere and that sometimes misery itself can seep into the walls of a house.

'Sit down, I'll make some tea.' Sheila Wootten spoke pleasantly enough as we entered the kitchen.

I sat down at the table on a hard-backed wooden chair while Miss Wootten filled a kettle and placed it on the gas cooker. The kitchen felt warmer and was neat, clean and tidy. Too tidy. Almost bare. The walls had been painted once in a colour that was probably magnolia but had now turned brownish beige and the only concessions to decoration were a calendar, unmarked, showing a picture of a greyhound and a potted fern that sat on the scrubbed pine table.

'Thank you for agreeing to see me,' I began. 'I've been worried about Vanessa for some time. She's been in hospital a few times recently...'

'Sugar?' she asked, although the water hadn't yet boiled.

'Oh—yes. One, thank you.'

There was no doubt I needed it. She turned her back then as she busied herself with preparing a tray for tea, and it seemed as if, by doing so, she was preparing herself psychologically for my questions.

Eventually, as she handed me tea in a flowered bone-china cup she said, 'Now then, Miss Kinsella, you were saying?'

I sipped the tea feigning pleasure; in reality it was milky, weak, and a great disappointment.

'Tell me about Vanessa,' I said quietly. 'Did she ever come here?'

'Come here! She lived here. This was the family home. She left when she was eighteen to go to London to do her nurse training.'

'And she never came back?'

'A few times. And for the funeral of course.'

'Funeral?'

'Mother died.'

'When was that?'

'More than ten years ago now.'

'And you haven't seen Vanessa since?'

Sheila Wootten, sitting opposite me, stared into her cup of tea for a few moments. 'No, thank God. And I don't want to see her ever again.' Now her eyes rested on mine, challenging me. Go on, argue with that, they seemed to say.

'Would you object to telling me why?' I asked.

'I'd prefer not to. Some wounds are too deep.'

I decided to try the guilt angle.

'I really don't want to intrude but my boss has entrusted me with the job of trying to sort out some of Vanessa's problems, and I should explain that the police are involved now.'

It was just as well that Sheila hadn't been holding a cup at the time. Her plump hands shook and she had to rest them on her thighs and then simultaneously her lower lip began to tremble and with it, her chins.

'Oh no,' she whispered, 'not after all this time. She couldn't have—she couldn't have.'

'Well, she has,' I said firmly. Wondering while I did so what the hell all this was about.

'I didn't think she would be so vindictive, so cruel. She promised. She promised . . .' Sheila's voice quavered and her eyes looked at me pleadingly as though I could change events both past and present.

'You tell me your version, Miss Wootten,' I said. 'And perhaps between us we can sort something out.'

'Yes. Yes,' she said slowly. 'I wouldn't want her story to be dragged up again. I wouldn't want people to know. It killed my mother, she had a heart attack. Not straight after, but she was never the same again. She lost her spirit, if you know what I mean.'

I nodded. 'Tell me what happened.'

Reluctantly and with one hand pressed to her cheek and her head held on one side Sheila began.

'We'd invited Vanessa to the engagement party—my engagement party, just a few close friends and a handful of relatives. She turned up the day of the party. I remember she wore a black dress but then I was so happy I didn't take much notice. We'd been going out together for five years and then Colin said it was time I had a proper ring and we planned to marry in a few months. We'd saved enough for a deposit on a house. I can't tell you how excited I was. After all, I'd met Colin late in life, I was nearing forty and we still hoped to start a family. Anyway, she turned up. Looking back she didn't say much. I thought she was jealous and that was why she seemed quiet. I just didn't realise how jealous . . .' She paused for a while as if trying to recall the day in even more detail.

'Go on,' I encouraged.

'The party was due to start at four. All the food was ready. Mother and I had worked really hard. We had an iced cake, champagne, a huge gammon and even a bit of smoked salmon. It was going to be a real celebration. I suggested the three of us have a drink before the guests came. Mother poured out the sherry and we stood here in this kitchen for a toast to the future...' Sheila's eyes now stared blankly into the distance of remembrance. She had forgotten I existed.

'And then?' I said quietly, trying to be politely intrigued without rushing her.

'And then,' she said dully, 'my dear sister opened her mouth. "You can't do it," she said. "You can't marry him." And at first I just thought she didn't want to lose me. Or that she was frightened Mother would expect her to return home. Then I realised there was more to it than that. She began to get hysterical, saying terrible things, telling lies. Mother had to sit down. I slapped Vanessa's face. I screamed at her to shut up but she wouldn't. On and on she went. Saying she felt guilty. She should have spoken up before. She was wrong to have been so frightened. Every word she said wrecked my dreams. Can you imagine how I felt? The guests were due to arrive, tears were streaming down my face, Mother was in a state of shock—and there *she* stood mouthing those awful lies. I wanted to kill her or die myself. I wanted a deep pit to swallow me up.'

Sheila's face had grown pale, her eyes seemed to have sunk and her bosom heaved with emotion. I sat tense and expectant and then in the silence I heard something fall above me. My eyes shot to the ceiling.

'It's the cat,' said Sheila but she said it too quickly, too glibly, with no surprise at all.

And then another noise came from above. This time, something seemed to roll across the floor.

'Who's up there?' I asked, in a far from normal voice.

Sheila's head slumped forward and she put her hands over her ears as the noise continued from above.

SEVENTEEN

SILENCE ABOVE THEN. But somehow that seemed more sinister than the noises.

How do the blind cope in a dark world where every sound is magnified, every noise a potential threat? Each creak of a floorboard or whine or whisper or moan could be some unimaginable horror, making you want to run and hide. But where, how?

Sheila Wootten looked up after a few moments and the calm expression on her face suggested she had made a decision.

'You stay here. I'll be back,' she said. And then she walked heavily and slowly up the stairs.

I listened carefully to her footsteps and heard the lock on a door opening; then came murmurings and a dragging noise and then more footsteps and this time an even slower and more cumbersome movement down the stairs.

The rain had begun to beat more heavily against the mean window-panes and the dark clouds had brought premature darkness. I simply waited, listening, and let my imagination work overtime as the lumbering sounds approached.

As the door opened Sheila appeared first, followed by a small man who seemed to be tucked under her arm. She began to half drag him to the kitchen chair. One of his legs was definitely not working. I stood up to help but she waved me away.

'I'm used to this,' she said, puffing with exertion. With a final effort she swung the man round and into the chair, and then dragged the chair nearer to the kitchen table. Then she too sank on to a chair.

'He doesn't come down often,' she said breathily.

The man sat with his head forward, thick black hair belying his poor condition. He had skin of a greyish-yellow pallor and a thin frame emphasised by the sweater he wore, pale blue and chunky and made for a much larger man. His short legs sported striped pyjama trousers worn with socks and brown shoes.

'This is Colin Tiffield,' Sheila announced suddenly and I felt ashamed to be so surprised at the love and pride in her voice.

'I didn't think that you...'

'We're not married,' said Sheila. 'He's been like this for two years. Brain-damaged in a car accident. That's how he lost his leg. He doesn't like the artificial one. That's what you heard. He throws it round the room when he's had enough of it. But he manages quite well really and he improves a little every day.' She looked towards Colin as if for confirmation. 'Don't you dear?'

Colin lifted his head slightly in response and I could see that although his eyes were grey and watery they were not totally blank. I smiled at him weakly and his head dropped again.

'More tea?' asked Sheila. 'Something to eat?'

'You're very kind,' I said. 'But I do have to get back to my office.'

Inside I was beginning to panic just a little. I had this feeling I might not be able to get away. Although of course they were a perfectly harmless couple, weren't they?

Sheila settled back in her chair. 'It's lovely having him here,' she said. 'He went abroad for a while and I was alone for a long time but then the accident happened and there was no one else to care for him and I was delighted to have him. I'm sure in a year or two he'll be back to normal.'

I nodded and smiled and then said, 'About Vanessa. You were telling me about the things she said at your engagement party.'

Nervously her eyes flicked to Colin but he seemed to have gone to sleep, his head, like a great heavy sphere, slumped on his chest.

'He does occasionally get violent,' she whispered. 'If he doesn't get his own way. He's small but strong.'

'Yes,' I said pointedly. 'And after the party?'

'Oh...the party...yes. Well, I was in shock as you can imagine. Mother managed to rally a bit and when the guests came she told them I'd been taken ill. That was true really. I had to lie on the bed for an hour to recover. Vanessa packed a bag and left straight away. She came back for the funeral. We didn't speak. I haven't spoken to her since. When someone says such terrible things you can't ever forgive them, can you?'

Very softly I asked, 'What exactly did she say, Miss Wootten?'

Sheila's blue eyes gazed for a few seconds somewhere beyond my shoulder. 'She said...she said Colin had...well, he'd interfered with her.'

'How do you mean—interfered?' I asked like a barrister feigning ignorance.

'*She* said'—the word 'she' Sheila spat out like an insult —'she said he'd raped her. And he'd been...using her ever since. For four years! Since she was fourteen. *That,* she said, was why she'd had to leave home at eighteen. She also said Colin had made death threats against her. She ranted on and on. She said if I married him she would go to the police and tell them everything.

I was forced to promise I wouldn't marry him. Can you believe it? Of course none of the things she said were true. And even if they were, she would have been leading him on, wouldn't she? I mean he's such a kind man. He used to pick her up from school and help with her homework. And drive her to friends' houses. He was a second father to her. Then she turned like a viper to tell all those lies just before the party. Little whore! I'm not surprised she needs social workers. She's mad, isn't she? I should pity her but I don't. I hope she's suffering as I've suffered. She always was the favourite, you know; the pretty one, leading on the boys. A lying devil, that's what she is. You shouldn't waste any of your time worrying about her. Anything she gets she deserves.'

Sheila's voice had grown louder and Colin's head lifted slowly as if in response. His eyes focused on me, a slow leering smile crossing his face and exposing yellow front teeth. Then he began to rock slightly, and, brain-damaged or not, I shuddered.

'I have to go now,' I said abruptly. 'I must get back.'

Sheila stood up in front of me, her large bosom like a shelf in my way.

'So soon?'

'Yes. The weather's bad and I'm not a very good night driver. I really will have to go.'

'She wants to go home, dear,' said Sheila, patting Colin on the shoulder.

There was no reaction.

'You could stay the night. I've got a spare room, it's all ready. Just needs some heating on.'

'Thank you. You've been very kind and helpful but I must go,' I repeated.

This time she moved back and gave me a weak smile. 'If you must you must. We get so few visitors stuck out here.'

That didn't surprise me.

But I was surprised at how good the cold and rain felt outside. It was nearly dark and puddles had collected in shiny pools and the air smelt of damp grass and manure—and freedom. Even the prospect of the drive home didn't daunt me. It seemed to me I had been away from Longborough for much longer than a few hours and it was only when the novelty of being out of the claustrophobic Maple Cottage began to wane that I fully realised what this meeting had meant.

Colin was not the main man. Vanessa's admirer had to be local. Someone unconnected with her family. Poor Vanessa seemed to me to be like a magnet for the odd and the deranged. Did he sense in her a victim mentality? Someone whose emotional hurt connected with hers as surely as if they had been wired together with the same traumatic impulses.

IT WAS NEARLY seven thirty by the time I neared Longborough. On the journey I'd made a deliberate effort not to think about my day. I'd wait until I got to Humberstones and then I could talk to Hubert. I wondered idly what Hubert would produce for his birthday meal and what a coincidence it was that I had thought of asking him for a meal just before he asked me. I'd already put a bottle of wine and a box of left-over Christmas chocolates on the back seat of the car. The only reason I hadn't eaten them was that they were soft centres. Hubert was a soft centre man, I was sure of that.

Humberstones was of course in darkness apart from the shaft of light that played on to the road from Hubert's flat. His part of the building sat adjacent to my office, separated by the walls of the adjoining house. The side entrance door was open and as I flicked on the light the fringe of the purple lamp shade trembled in the draught.

I walked quickly through to Hubert's staircase and was reassured when he appeared at the top silhouetted in the pinkish glow that came from the room beyond. He wore a grey polo neck sweater and slickly creased grey trousers.

'This is the lounge,' he said when I reached him, and he stretched out his arm proudly to encompass the room.

It was indeed a room to be proud of. The walls were in silver regency stripe and the lighting from black-stemmed lamps with cerise shades gave the room a soft and friendly glow. Two sofas sat facing each other, opulent in cream with cushions edged in gold braid. It was a pity that on the coffee table, a magazine, *Funeral Director,* peeked out from under *Shoes Through The Ages*. A log fire burned steadily in a splendid mantled grate and at first I thought the flames were real, not gas.

'It's lovely, Hubert,' I said as I kissed him on the cheek and wished him happy birthday.

'You haven't seen it all yet,' he said as he led me to the room next door.

This was obviously the dining-room with kitchen attached, and judging by the savoury smell something delicious lurked in his ultra-modern cooker, so bright with lights and infra-red plates it looked primed and ready for take-off.

An arch separated the kitchen area from the dining part and a round table in the middle had been laid with a white lace cloth and what looked like real silver cutlery. Half a dozen pink and white carnations stood in a narrow stemmed vase and by its side a bottle of Sancerre stood chilling in an ice-bucket.

Just for a moment I felt a tinge of sadness for us both. For Hubert because he had tried so hard and for me because rarely had anyone gone to this amount of trouble before. Dave's idea of a treat had been to come home before closing time, with a bottle of cheap red plonk and two vindaloos...

'Sherry?' Hubert was saying.

'I'd love one.'

We drank the sherry quickly then sat down to eat garlic mushrooms with giant prawns, eased down with two glasses each of Sancerre. The main course was pheasant in red wine which we washed down with more red wine. By this time Maple Cottage seemed very far away and I told Hubert about my visit as if it had been no more unusual than a visit to Tesco.

'Where does that leave you, then?' he asked.

'Back to square one, Hubert,' I said. 'I'll have to review my paltry list of suspects.'

'Maybe it's someone you haven't met yet. Perhaps you should make more door-to-door enquiries; perhaps you should—'

'Perhaps I should do a lot of things but I'm full of wine and food and as a consequence my investigative powers have been blunted.'

'You're not drunk,' said Hubert, 'you managed to say investigative.'

Dessert was a pavlova with raspberries which I recognised as an M and S special but it tasted good, better than good with the Sauternes Hubert produced to round off the meal.

Hubert insisted we left the washing-up for the dishwasher and that we should collapse in the lounge.

'Are you going to tell me how old you are, Hubert?' I asked as I sank into one of his sofas.

He smiled, happy with food and drink. 'I'm fifty.'

Drink can make me maudlin. The big 5—0 and only a lodger for a guest. 'Oh, Hubert, I'm sorry,' I said before I could stop myself. Fifty seemed so old. Thirty was bad enough but fifty!

'In this world,' said Hubert, peering at me through alcohol-misted eyes, 'we should be grateful for another day. Lots of people I know have popped off early...'

'Well, you would know a lot, wouldn't you... in your line of work.'

And then I began to laugh at Hubert's serious face until he too began to laugh. He suggested brandy and we drank that slowly and giggled about nothing in particular and slumped into contented semi-dozes in front of the TV until the phone rang.

I went to the bathroom as Hubert answered the phone. And what a bathroom! A circular bath, nearly as big as my office bedroom, sat like a giant shell, surrounded by walls of expensive tiling and with gold-plated taps that sparkled like a jeweller's window. And I had to wash in the sink!

Hubert had finished on the phone when I returned and he looked like a man who had just dropped his keys down a drain.

'What's the matter?' I asked. 'What's happened?'

'It's bad news,' he said dramatically. 'Well, it's a complication anyway.'

'Tell me.'

'That was a woman I know, a neighbour of Vanessa's. She was giving me a tip-off.'

'Yes, Hubert,' I said impatiently.

'Well it seems . . . it seems . . . Vanessa has just been arrested.' And then he added, 'For the murder of Paul Oakby.'

EIGHTEEN

'ARRESTED?' I echoed, and then realised that wasn't the real issue. Paul Oakby was dead! I felt slightly sick as the alcohol I'd drunk started defying the laws of gravity. 'How was he killed?' I managed to ask.

Hubert shook his head, 'I've no idea. The tip-off was a bit vague.'

'I'll have to go to the police station now—this minute,' I said, mild panic making me imagine that I could feel my adrenalin levels rising like a tide to join up with waves of red and white wine.

I must have looked wild and keen because Hubert said, 'Now you just calm down, Kate. You can't drive. I'll ring for a mini-cab. You just sit down for a minute and suck a mint.'

I sucked the extra strong he gave me while I waited impatiently for the mini-cab to arrive.

Somehow Oakby's murder was far more horrific than May's: he was strong, tough and aggressive and whoever killed him I presumed was equally so—and violent—and getting desperate.

Hubert tut-tutted a bit and I said how sorry I was that I'd spoilt his day but I'd had a lovely time.

'You come back here,' said Hubert. 'Don't go driving back to Farley Wood this late. I'll wait up for you. The police will keep you hanging around for ages.'

'There's no need for that, Hubert. I think I can find my way back to my own office.'

He scowled, creasing his forehead into deep horizontal lines and said gruffly, 'It's still my birthday and I want to know what's going on.'

I patted his shoulder in a gesture of compliance. 'You win, Hubert. I'll be back and I'll tell you all about it.'

He smiled then. 'I've had a great birthday, Kate—the best for a long time.'

He didn't seem to mind that it had ended in a murder and the arrest of my only client. Perhaps he thought it added an interesting dimension to his celebration of fifty years.

THE POLICE STATION was warm, the reception area buzzing with activity. People coming and going and then coming again. The phone rang incessantly and it was so busy that I simply sat down in a corner by the cactus and prepared for a long wait. I spent half an hour watching the faces of those walking to and fro. The police surgeon, Dr Benfleet, was one of those on his way out and he stopped and sat down on the chair beside me. His rounded cheeks glowed with either excitement or effort and he seemed a little breathless and spoke in a whisper.

'Nasty one this is,' he said. 'Your client, isn't she?'

I nodded. 'Have you seen her?'

'I most certainly have. She's in a bit of a state. It's not every day you find a dead man in your lounge, is it?'

'But why have they arrested Vanessa?' I asked in a whisper as the desk Sergeant with the large head appeared behind the counter and caught sight of me.

'She's not arrested,' replied Benfleet, 'just helping with enquiries.'

The desk Sergeant was by now signalling for me to approach the counter.

Dr Benfleet smiled at me sympathetically and stood up as I did. 'Take care,' he said.

The desk Sergeant couldn't drum up a smile sympathetic or otherwise. He seemed to be in a state of harassed anxiety. 'Come on, Miss Kinsella,' he said. 'CID want to have a word with you.'

'Sounds ominous,' I replied.

He frowned at me. My attempt to lighten his mood obviously hadn't worked and I realised the alcohol I'd drunk had probably dulled for me the full realisation of what had happened. Someone had, after all, murdered a policeman. I just wasn't prepared to believe that Vanessa could have been responsible.

Inspector Hook's expression of grim determination quite unnerved me as I entered the interview room. Potted plants and paintings were definitely not fashionable for interrogation purposes. The room was bare, save for a table and two chairs, and windowless. As grim as Hook's face and as I closed the door behind me I felt guilt spread over me as rapidly as a blush. I haven't done anything wrong, I told myself. I couldn't have prevented it—could I?

'Sit down,' said Hook.

I sat down and smiled, trying to look as innocent as possible. I was innocent but somehow I didn't feel it.

'You know of course what's happened,' said Hook.

I nodded. 'Paul Oakby has been found murdered.'

Hook stared at me. 'There's murder and murder,' he said with raised brows.

I wasn't quite sure of the correct response to that, so I just said, 'Yes.'

'Do you know how he died?' asked Hook, leaning towards me across the desk in a gesture I found intimidating.

'I don't know anything about his death,' I explained. 'Just that he's dead.'

'Who told you he was dead?'

'Just one of my sources. I can't disclose who, can I?'

He didn't comment but he took from his pocket a notebook and pen and then asked, 'Where exactly were you this evening?'

Just for a moment I hesitated. 'Am I to understand I'm a suspect, Inspector?'

'I'm waiting,' said Hook irritably.

'I was at Humberstones. I've been there since just after seven thirty. Mr Humberstone can verify that.'

'No need to get agitated, Kate,' said Hook, giving me, along with my name, a glimmer of a smile. 'We're looking into every possibility, everyone's a suspect when one of ours is killed.'

'Are you going to tell me what happened?' I asked.

'This is my interview,' said Hook. 'I ask the questions. You answer them.'

'I'll try.'

'Good. Do you own a gun?'

I had to smile at that. 'Of course I don't own a gun. Why would I want a gun?'

Hook didn't smile and then I realised why.

'Oakby was shot?' I asked in surprise.

He nodded. 'Point-blank range in the face. Very, very vicious. The person we're looking for is a real nutter. A head case.'

I didn't say anything. What was there to say?

After a few moments Hook said, 'We haven't got very far with Miss Wootten. She's like a zombie. Frederic Tissot was more help. It seems they went out together, Tissot spinning his wife some yarn about late-night seminars. Anyway they went out for a curry and a drink and then stayed chatting in the car for a while. They were seen by a PC about ten thirty in the town centre. Tissot dropped Miss Wootten off at her house. They both say he didn't go inside at this point. She was alone when she found Oakby. Dead. Splattered against the walls of her lounge. The door was open and she found him almost immediately. The doc's not sure how long he'd been dead but rigor mortis hadn't set in and she'd only been out since eight. So time of death is set tentatively for between eight and eleven. But the guess is round about ten. Oakby didn't put up much of a struggle. I expect he was taken by surprise. He just got both barrels in the face.'

I was glad I was sitting down. I couldn't think straight. My voice came out croaky and strained. 'How did he get in?' I asked, remembering he still had a key.

'Who?'

'Either of them.'

Hook shrugged. 'We're not sure yet. A plywood board had been removed from a window by the kitchen door. The forensic team are still busy in the house and likely to be for hours yet.'

'Did the neighbours hear anything?'

Hook's irritation returned as unremitting as waves of colic. 'That's one question too many, Kate. But I'll tell you because I don't want you doing any more snooping. Only one neighbour heard anything and she thought it was a car backfiring. No one saw anything because they had their curtains drawn. I suppose they were watching the news.'

'Just one more question, Inspector,' I said in a hopefully wheedling way. 'Have you any firm suspects?'

Hook shrugged despondently. 'Not as yet, but I can tell you this: we won't rest until we find them. If necessary we'll interview every man in Longborough.'

'I ...'

'Yes?' said Hook impatiently.

'There is someone Vanessa mentioned; has she given you a name yet?'

There was no immediate answer. Hook flicked open his notebook wordlessly and waited with poised pen.

'Vanessa thinks the man responsible is a Colin Tiffield. But... I've been to see him today and he's physically and mentally disabled. It couldn't be him.'

'We'll check him out anyway,' said Hook as I gave him the address.

After a short silence I guessed I'd been dismissed but then Hook said, 'There's something else. A message was written on the mirror, in Oakby's blood. "YOU NEXT, V", it said. So your client will have to be well guarded for a while.'

As I stood up I felt my knees struggle to keep me upright.

'You okay?' asked Hook, taking me by the arm. 'You look a bit shaky.'

'I'm ... fine,' I said. 'It's just been a shock, that's all.'

'We may need to speak to you again, Kate. Where will we find you?'

'I'll be at Humberstones.'

'Good. A maniac is on the loose. It might be better if you stay there. Keep a low profile too; he may have plans for ... well ... just be careful. Remember we're the professionals.'

'Yes, of course, Inspector. Would it be possible for me to see Vanessa?'

Hook shrugged and then said with weary tolerance, 'If you get any more out of her than us—good luck. She's definitely not telling us everything but she is in shock of course. Forensic say she's clean, and there was no sign of the weapon. She has been telling us for ages that some-one is out to get her: perhaps we should have taken more notice.' Then he added, 'Come on, I'll take you to her.'

I felt a little reassured that guilt was being shared round but when I saw Vanessa even that vanished. She looked ill. Pale and exhausted, she sat slumped over a table in another bare interview room. She wore a blue dress with a dropped waist and the hooped earrings had been re-placed by pearl drops. A policewoman sat by her and in front of them on the table were a half empty cup of tea and a plate of curled-at-the-edges sandwiches.

She looked up as I entered, one hand supporting her head in tired resignation. Her blue eyes, dull with misery and exhaustion, stared at me and she tried to smile in recognition but she failed, her eyes instead filling with tears.

Hook signalled for the young WPC who sat beside her to leave and as she closed the door I sat down and reached out for Vanessa's hand. It was icy cold.

'You're leaving here, Vanessa,' I said, 'with police protection. You'll be safe.'

She continued to stare at me with a look as cold as her hand. A stare that said I'd failed her, everyone had failed her.

'Poor Paul,' she said. 'That should have been me on the floor. He would have been expecting me. He was hiding in the house with a gun. Did you know that?' Her voice trailed off hoarsely, a dull monotone, all emotion gone. 'He said he'd kill me. And he will.'

'When did he say he'd kill you?' I asked.

'A long time ago.'

'You mean Colin Tiffield?'

'Yes.'

'But it can't be him, Vanessa. I've seen him today. He's a physical and mental wreck. It couldn't be him.'

'I shouldn't have told,' she said dully, as though she hadn't heard me. 'He's mad. He's always been mad.'

I hugged her as she began to sob and after a while Hook signalled for me to go. As I left the WPC came back. I don't think Vanessa knew I'd gone.

The desk Sergeant kindly rang for a mini-cab to take me back to Humberstones.

'Best not to walk,' he said. 'Not till he's found.'

A plain black four-door car turned up in a few minutes, driven by a reassuringly cheerful man who managed to tell me three very unfunny knock-knock jokes on the short journey back.

'Keep smiling, duck,' he said as I paid him outside Humberstones.

Hubert must have watched me arrive because he came down to the side door to let me in.

'I bolted the door,' he said, 'just in case.'

'Very wise, Hubert. In the circumstances.'

'Which are?'

'Dire, Hubert, dire!'

Upstairs in his flat Hubert made cocoa and we sat quietly sipping for a while. I knew he was longing to ask me what had happened but I needed time to think events through. So far in this investigation I had managed to accomplish—zilch. No, that wasn't quite true. I had found a one-legged man who had once abused Vanessa. Other than that—nothing. Perhaps it was even my fault that Paul Oakby had been murdered. He had been trying to get information for me. Was that why he'd gone to the house?

'You going to tell me then?' said Hubert, swirling the last bit of cocoa round in his mug.

'He was shot, Hubert, in the face.'

'Poor sod,' said Hubert. 'May he rest in peace.'

'Amen. What do I do now?'

'Well, there's no need to sound so defeated,' said Hubert. 'I take it Vanessa hasn't been arrested so you've just got to come up with another suspect.'

'You make that sound easy. Anyway I've given the police a few names and I expect they'll be interviewing every male she's ever said good morning to. It's just a feeling that somewhere I've missed something vital. Vanessa was so convinced it was him.'

Hubert stood up then and took the empty from my hand. 'You go to bed, Kate. You look knackered. In the morning you'll have one of your ideas.'

I watched him carefully to see if he was being sarcastic but he didn't even blink.

'Good night, Hubert,' I said. 'And many happy returns.'

My 'bedroom' seemed claustrophobically small after being in Hubert's spacious flat and I lay awake for a long time trying to think what to do next. Should I just leave everything to the police? Would they do any better?

I dreamt that I was on rifle practice but I wasn't doing the shooting—I was the target. A big red cross was painted on my forehead and I was strapped to a huge dartboard and Hook and Roade were taking aim but instead of the merciful release of a fatal bullet they missed every time.

I woke up suddenly, hot and alert. I threw off the duvet and then heard a slight noise on the stairs outside. Soft and shuffling. I held my breath as though silence would make the sound stop, but it didn't. Someone was moving about outside. Sliding out of bed I tiptoed to the door. It was unlocked. He could get in. I listened with my ear to the door, trying to breathe in short shallow breaths so that he couldn't hear me. The footsteps—slow, deliberate—were approaching my door.

NINETEEN

My ear was still pressed against the door when the knocking began.

Murderers don't knock on doors. I swung open the door sharply—there stood Hubert, smiling. In one hand he held a mug and in the other an airmail letter.

'For God's sake, Hubert!' I burst out. 'Why on earth are you creeping about in the middle of the night? You could cause sudden death like that.'

'It is eight o'clock. I brought you coffee and a letter,' he said, cheerfully for him, and then added just as cheerfully, 'I like your nightshirt. I've got one like that.'

'Oh good,' I said. 'You'd better come in.'

I guided Hubert through the darkness of the 'bedroom' to my office and left him while I dressed quickly.

When I returned he had pulled up the blinds and watery sunshine filtered on to my desk, catching speckles of dust that danced in the column of light. I watched it for a happy moment, glad that all that had terrorised me in the night had been dreams and Hubert's footsteps.

Now he sat back in the swivel chair and handed me the letter.

'It's from your Mum, isn't it? I'm pleased she's written to you. I thought you and she had stopped writing.'

I opened the letter eagerly. The first few lines convinced me she was well. She had spent the summer watching the talent on Bondi beach and waitressing in the evenings. I thought she was a bit old for that sort of thing but she certainly seemed to be enjoying the adolescence she must have missed . . .

'She's all right is she?' asked Hubert.

'She's fine,' I said, folding up the letter half read to save till later when I was alone.

'Good,' said Hubert. 'Families should always keep in touch. Nothing's worth falling out with family.'

'We haven't fallen out. We just don't write to each other very often.'

I'd drunk half my coffee and was trying to plan my next move when Hubert said, 'Have you made up your mind what to do next?'

I sighed. 'I won't even be able to do any door-to-door enquiries. The police will be all over Percival Road like . . .'

'Ants over a dung hill?' suggested Hubert.

'Precisely. I could, I suppose, manage to find one or two patients and question them again. Mrs Spokes might know more . . .' I tailed off. I wasn't convinced. It all seemed so hopeless. I'd failed Vanessa and Paul had died.

Hubert must have noticed I seemed down because he said, 'I'd come with you if I could but I've got two funerals today and two tomorrow. The fridge is chock-a-block.'

I feigned surprise but really I was getting used to the ordinariness of being in a house for the dead. 'Oh, Hubert!' I said. 'You make the deceased sound like so many tubs of ice-cream.'

'Be a lot easier, wouldn't it?' he said with a grin. But he quickly grew glum-faced again. 'Now just you take care, Kate. This lunatic might decide to come after *you* now that Vanessa is safe. It would be better if you didn't go about on your own.'

'Nonsense,' I said. But I knew it wasn't.

BEFORE GOING TO Mrs Spokes I tracked down Andrew Norten. Not that I actually saw him. His landlady informed me he'd gone to Saudi Arabia but she expected him back in a year!

After that Mrs Spokes's caustic greeting of, 'Oh, it's you again,' seemed quite promising.

I was invited in, though, when I explained I'd come merely for a chat.

'I'm doing well lately,' she said. 'The police, Fred, even the vicar. Sit yourself down and I'll get you a bite to eat.'

Despite my protestations in moments I had set before me a pot of tea and a huge cheese roll. In my honour she also turned off the sound of the television but she still positioned herself in front of the set and stared ahead.

'You young girls don't eat enough,' she admonished suddenly. 'And you don't wear proper knickers.'

Between mouthfuls I said, 'You've heard about the murder, I suppose.'

'Course I have. Longborough's never had so much excitement. I bet the TV cameras will be here today. How's Vanessa taking it?'

'She's in shock.'

'Poor little bugger. Bound to happen in the end though, wasn't it?'

'What was?'

'Something like this. A girl as pretty as she is is bound to cause trouble.'

'What do you think happened, then?'

Mrs Spokes shrugged and rearranged her floral apron. 'I dunno for sure but perhaps that Paul Oakby saw someone in the house, went to investigate and POW! he gets his head blown off.'

'Why would a burglar shoot him?'

'Aren't you supposed to be a detective?'

'Well, yes...'

'Huh! You don't look very tough to me.'

'It's more brains than brawn you need, Mrs Spokes.'

She gave me what my mother would have called an 'old-fashioned look' and said nothing.

I was on my second cup of tea when Mrs Spokes said, 'Funny the way she got so scared about that bloke who was supposed to be following her. She had boyfriends but I don't think a single one of them made her happy, you know. Not for long anyway. I reckon...' Mrs Spokes tailed off and folded her short arms so that they rested on the roundness that combined both breasts and stomach.

'What do you reckon, Mrs Spokes?'

'I think there's only one man who is right for her in Longborough and she turned him down.'

'Who was that?'

'I never told the police though. Well, they'd suspect their own mother, wouldn't they?'

'Who was it?'

'Dr Hiding of course. He'd taken a real shine to her but she said no. He's a bit of a dark horse that one.'

'Mrs Spokes,' I said trying to sound outraged, 'surely you don't think Dr Hiding is capable of murder?'

'No, duck, I don't think he'd do anything violent but he is tuppence short of a shilling, isn't he?'

I tried not to smile. 'Anyone else who may have asked her out?'

'Let me think,' she said. 'There was someone. A few months ago. She didn't say his name but she seemed surprised if you know what I mean. Like he was too young for her or drawing his pension.'

'Did she say where she'd met him?'

Mrs Spokes stared into her gas fire for a moment. 'I think he was a patient. Perhaps she didn't like what he'd got? Perhaps it was catching.'

I left Mrs Spokes having promised I'd visit again and drove straight to the Health Centre. Surely, I thought, Dr Hiding would be aware of any local disturbed man. Not that David Hiding was a bench-mark for normality.

I was lucky: he had just seen his last patient of the morning and was sitting in his consulting room with the door wide open, staring at a pile of correspondence on his desk. He looked up as I entered.

'Ah, I was meditating, Miss Kinsella. Finding new strength from the Almighty. Do you ever pray?'

'When I'm scared.'

'I see. You believe God will help you in times of trouble?'

'Not exactly. I'm just hedging my bets.'

He sighed, as if seeing I would stay a heathen and flourished a cardigan-covered arm towards a chair. As I sat down he said, 'How may I help?'

'It's about Vanessa Wootten.'

'Ah, yes. She's getting over the shock, I hope. A terrible thing to happen here.'

'Pretty bad anywhere,' I agreed.

'Yes. Yes. Of course,' he said irritably. He lowered his glasses to the end of his nose and stared at me.

'You were quite friendly with Vanessa, I believe?' I asked abruptly.

His eyes widened. 'Of course. She worked here. We were on good terms.'

'Asking out terms?'

Hiding put his glasses back on properly. 'We didn't have a relationship if that is what you are implying.'

'But you would have liked one? You did fancy her?'

'Fancy is a crude word, Miss Kinsella. I liked her, that's all.'

'You did ask her out though, didn't you?' I persisted.

'Yes,' he said wearily. 'I did ask her out once or twice. She refused. There isn't much else to say.'

'For you, perhaps, but I have heard that a patient may also have asked her out and been refused.'

Hiding shrugged. 'She is popular. That doesn't surprise me.'

My questions had made Dr Hiding edgy and defensive. Now I tried a different approach. I smiled.

'I'm sorry about the questions, David. I've come to you because I'm sure Vanessa would have confided in you about her past. And I'm sure you'll agree we need to do everything we can to bring the murderer to justice.'

There was silence then as if he were wrestling with his Hippocratic oath or his conscience, or both. 'You know about her family background?'

I nodded. 'Yes. Well, from her sister's viewpoint.'

'Vanessa was undoubtedly abused as a child and is terrified of the man, but as for him following her for years I think that is a delusory manifestation of her past fears and misery.'

That sounded so convincing that it took me a moment to reply. 'But what about this other fellow? The man who blasted Paul Oakby to death. That's not delusory manifestation, is it? Or poor May Brigstock. I've met the man Vanessa is so afraid of, and he's not capable of murder.'

'Have *you* any idea who this man is, then?' asked Hiding.

'No,' I said. 'That's why I've come to you. Vanessa only gave me a very vague description of the man and at the time she thought she knew who he was. He's medium height, medium build, drives a car and seems to have access to others, and he owns or can get hold of a shotgun.'

David Hiding smirked a little at that.

'What's so funny?' I asked.

'Kate, my dear, this is a country town. There are shotguns all over the place. The farmers, members of the gun clubs and rich Londoners doing a bit of shooting at weekends.'

'And they all have a licence?'

'I'm sure they do. I'm often asked for character references by the police.'

'Any lately?'

'Not that I can remember. Of course the other partners may have. I'd have to check our records and then go through the computer—we're in the middle of changing over to a fully computerised system at the moment.'

'How long will that take?'

'God willing, only a few months.'

'Months,' I echoed.

Hiding smiled. 'I might have luck with the manual records.'

'Thank you, David. One last question; well, the same question. The one you avoided answering.'

'Which is?'

'Do you know of any admirers Vanessa may have had in the practice, particularly unstable ones?'

An expression of reluctance passed across the doctor's face. 'Oh, very well,' he said. 'Young Christopher Collicot has a crush on Vanessa. It's been going on some time and now it's interfering with his studies. His parents even know about it. He is apt to hang about the Health Centre just so that he can catch a glimpse of her. But I can assure you he is perfectly sane and of a non-violent disposition.'

'Being in love changes people,' I said. But surely not that much?

As I drove back towards Humberstones I reasoned that it was better to have one suspect than none and that perhaps I should keep a sharp eye on young Christopher. I'd been so convinced that the past was all that mattered in Vanessa's life that it was a shock to realise that I had been concentrating only on the past few weeks. Maybe Vanessa had cried wolf once too often and then when somebody really was after her no one believed her. Just as her sister hadn't believed her.

I'd just got out of the car and had turned to get my shoulder bag from the front passenger seat when I heard Hubert's voice: 'Kate, you coming my way?'

I turned in surprise to see Hubert directly in front of me. 'Which way's that, Hubert?'

'Towards the Swan of course.'

'Oh all right.'

'Don't force yourself.'

'I won't then.'

'Go on, Kate, be a sport. A drink will do you good. Perk you up.'

'I'm perked enough, thank you.'

But insistently Hubert stuck out his arm and I shrugged in defeat and looped my arm through his and we walked along the High Street to the safe haven and soft lights of the Swan.

'We must look a queer couple,' I said.

'Not as queer as some,' he answered as he opened the door to the lounge bar.

The lunchtime trade was, as usual these days, less than brisk. There were only two other customers and Hubert was soon back.

'Here's your drink,' he announced placing half a pint of cider in front of me.

'I'm still reduced to cider, I see. I should have bought the drinks.'

'Brandy will knock you out,' said Hubert knowingly.

'You're probably right,' I said, sipping the liquid and trying to look pleased with it.

'What's wrong, Kate? You look like a woman whose knicker elastic has just given way in the High Street.'

'Hubert,' I said, 'you've changed. When I first came to Humberstones you seemed shy and retiring. You didn't swear and knickers wasn't a word in your vocabulary.'

Hubert smiled as if I'd paid him a compliment. 'The cider's reviving you, I can see that. You're back on form.'

I smiled. 'I'm only pretending, Hubert. I'm at a loss. I've failed on this one. Where do I start looking for the invisible man? The gun could be a big lead but Dr Hiding says guns are common round here.'

'Well he should know—he's got one.'

'How do you know?'

'I've seen him out shooting rabbits.'

'And him a Christian,' I said. 'You'll be telling me next the vicar's got one.'

'He has. Shoots the crows that try to feed on his garden produce. He's a very keen gardener. Has to be, I suppose. Vicars don't earn much, do they? His wife only does voluntary work for the disabled, they have a son to keep and the rectory must cost a fortune to heat.'

'Don't tell me they both shoot as well.'

'Not that I know of,' said Hubert. 'Mind you, I was surprised that Christopher went off to theological college.'

'Why? He seems just the type to me.'

'He went through a bit of a wild stage. I heard it rumoured he was in trouble with the police once.'

'What was he supposed to have done?'

'I'm not sure but I think it was taking and driving away. Anyway the police didn't press charges so it couldn't have been very serious, could it?'

'No, I suppose not,' I agreed. 'Dr Crippen was a mild-looking man, wasn't he?'

'What are you talking about, Kate?'

'It's just that young Christopher is besotted with Vanessa... I was just thinking about appearances being deceptive.'

'Well,' said Hubert, 'you could always try to get an invitation to the rectory. To eliminate him from your enquiries.'

'Perhaps you could come with me, Hubert. I might need to have a look round, especially Christopher's bedroom. You could keep the family occupied.'

Hubert looked undecided. 'Not after the last time I helped you. That dog, do you remember?'

'It was only a scratch, Hubert, don't be such a baby.'

'I'm surprised you haven't heard.'

'Heard what?'

'Christopher's got a dog. A Rottweiler puppy.'

But he's not the type, I was about to say. But perhaps he was.

TWENTY

VANESSA PHONED that evening. She felt much better but she was bored with reading and playing patience.

'Have you made any progress, Kate?'

I had to admit I hadn't, but I said, 'The police are doing everything they can. It won't be much longer.'

'I do hope not,' she said. 'I want to go back home. This flat is quite comfortable but it's not home. I don't think I can stand it much longer. The police have visited my sister. HE was there of course, but they assure me he isn't capable of being Paul's killer.'

'All this will soon end, Vanessa, I promise you. He'll be found.'

'I hope you're right,' she said, 'I really do.'

It was true about the police. They really had been trying. Door-to-door enquiries had been extensive; they'd even put a short piece on TV's *Crime Watch*. According to Hubert that had resulted in hundreds of phone-calls but mostly from oddballs who either hated the police or were overly keen to confess to almost any murder on offer.

I'd almost forgotten about the fête but Mrs Morcott rang to remind me. 'Could you be there by twelve thirty? We've rather more jumble than I anticipated.'

'I'll be there,' I said, grateful that I'd have something to do. And perhaps I'd be able to have a word with the vicar's wife about Christopher, who was beginning to become rather more promising as a suspect. Although owning a Rottweiler and having a crush on a pretty young

woman seemed thin grounds for suspicion; for a vicar's
son anyway.

THE WI HALL, a converted brick-built barn with a red
corrugated roof, was within walking distance of my house
but the weather had taken a turn for the wintry and snow
was promised, so I decided to drive. The small parking
area was nearly full and I couldn't fail to notice the black
van with dark windows parked nearest to the door.

Inside, the activity looked like preparations for the
immediate civil defence of Farley Wood. Mrs Morcott
was valiantly trying to organise everyone.

'Over there, dear...that's it, Mrs Warton, all the cakes
and biscuits on one table...Mrs Goody, that's right,
knick-knacks and haberdashery on the white elephant
table.'

She looked up as I came into the hall. 'Ah, Miss Kinsella, good of you to come early. Your table is in the corner; there's a lot of sorting out to do, I'm afraid. Mrs
Collicot will give you a hand though.'

As I began to wade through the boxes and worried-
looking helpers Verna Collicot touched my arm. 'It's arriving by the car-load,' she whispered. 'At this rate we'll
have at least three trestle tablesful.'

I glanced from her pale worried face to the corner and
the mound of old clothes that was already at table level.
'It's like something from a horror movie, isn't it?' I said,
refusing to be panicked by the sight of piles of old and, I
suspected, smelly clothes.

Verna gave me a weak smile. I had seen her very occasionally walking round the village but this was the first
time I'd spoken to her. She had a smaller nose than her
son and more chin but her lips were equally thin. Her
hair, fair but tinged with grey, was straight and wispy and

her skin had a faintly mottled appearance as though she went out unprotected in all weathers. She wore a grey cardigan, darned at the elbows, and she wore a white blouse pinned at the neck with a tiny blue butterfly brooch. A gold cross lay just below the butterfly. Her skirt was of faded navy, thick, with an elasticated waist that made her slim figure look bunched in the middle. Could this genteel, fragile lady possibly be the mother of a murderer? I wondered. But since a murderer's mother is a subject I know less about than village fêtes, I kept a very open mind.

'Would you sort out the men's clothing?' Verna asked. 'Just pile the better-looking articles to the front to attract people. I'll do the ladies' table.'

I began gathering up an armful and picking out the jackets and shirts that looked reasonable and folding them quickly but carefully as I put them to the front of the trestle. The noise in the hall gradually reduced to a gentle buzz of conversation as the various stalls became organised.

Verna and I spoke little. Occasionally she murmured, 'That's nice,' and 'What do you think of this?' as a dress or a blouse took her fancy. I noticed that if I seemed to approve she placed the article in a carrier bag at her feet. When she realised I was aware of it she blushed and whispered, 'I have to alter them a bit so people don't recognise them, but I can't afford to buy new clothes.'

'I'll see if I can find something for Christopher,' I said.

'Oh, thank you. He's been off sick now from college such a long time I sometimes doubt he'll go back. I'm afraid he's clothed entirely from jumble sales. The villagers don't notice men's clothing so much, do they?'

I smiled and continued searching for clothes with Christopher appeal.

At last our tables were covered but we still had piles around our feet. A musty old clothes smell seemed to surge up like an invisible cloud but that didn't diminish the satisfaction of the organised tables.

'Well done, you two,' said Mrs Morcott, advancing on us with mugs of tea. 'I hope Verna's prepared you for the onslaught.'

I looked questioningly at Verna.

She smiled. 'I didn't want you to run away, but it can be ... well ... really awful. The pushing and shoving and grabbing and arguing. But don't take any notice, Kate. As for prices, we used to vary them a bit but we don't any more. There was too much bargaining going on. Now it's twenty pence each item and no reductions; well, not until about four thirty.'

I drank my tea and at just before two everyone manned their stalls and stood ready and alert.

'Right, everyone,' called out Mrs Morcott. 'I'll start the countdown. Good luck and courage to you all. Ten, nine, eight ...'

As she got to one she took a deep breath and opened the door. People swarmed in, most of them seeming to make for our stall and suddenly my carefully arranged clothes were snatched up, yanked, held up, seams were pulled, labels examined, money thrust at me, bags demanded. And the noise of excited bargain-hunters assaulted my ears so that I couldn't hear myself saying 'Who's next?' or 'Thank you'.

It was possibly the worst few hours of my life. A fight nearly broke out between two elderly women who wanted the same skirt and as one thrust it at me the other grabbed my arm.

'You're too fat for that, you silly cow,' said one.

'Oh no, I'm not, you old bag.'

'Ladies, please,' I said, which I thought would mollify them. It didn't.

'You stay out of this, you stuck-up bitch,' said the younger of the two.

Dragging me into their squabble seemed to dampen their keenness to fight and angrily one said, 'It's far too big for me anyway. I'd have to alter it and I've gone off the colour. It's an old woman's skirt, I don't want it.'

Which left the victorious owner feeling no doubt fat as a house and with a skirt she'd never enjoy wearing.

Eventually five o'clock came and the last few customers had left, leaving me in a state of post-fête shock. Although Verna sighed with relief she seemed hardened to it. Mrs Morcott supplied more tea and we began the wearisome task of clearing up the debris.

I was in the middle of bagging up the left-over jumble when Christopher walked in. 'Like a hand, Mother?' he asked. He wore a black baseball cap, black tee-shirt and blue jeans. He smiled shyly at me. 'Is there any news of Vanessa?'

'A phone-call,' I said. 'She's getting over the shock now and raring to come home.'

'That's good,' he said, smiling. 'I've been praying for her.'

With Christopher's help, what was left on our tables was soon cleared into black plastic bags and put in the black van outside. At one point I heard Verna and Christopher whispering together but since I heard the word 'shirts' I think it was merely a discussion of the spoils of jumble.

I was almost ready to go when Verna said, 'You will stay for supper, won't you? It's Indian, all prepared, it won't take long to put together. Christopher cooks very well.'

'I'd love to,' I said, never having been known to refuse a meal.

THE ROTTWEILER PUPPY came bounding towards us as
the front door was opened. Round and fat and happy.
Thankfully it didn't bark, just gyrated in ecstatic shaking movements.

'She's called Janey,' said Christopher proudly as he
bent down to pat her.

'Do take her out for a walk, Christopher,' said Verna.
'Kate and I would love a sherry, wouldn't we?'

I nodded. As I followed Verna from the hall I noticed
how threadbare the carpets were. And although the
staircase rose majestically with a well-polished banister,
the stair carpet was bald in patches.

'Do make yourself comfortable,' said Verna, showing
me into a sitting-room that was remarkable for its air of
defeat. An old TV, black and white, I guessed, faced towards three high-backed chairs with varying floral cov-
ers faded and torn in places. One wall was covered by
shelves of books, all serious tomes judging by the cov-
ers. The curtains at the bay window were of a nonde-
script beige pattern with matching pelmet that was
beginning to come away from the wall. Only the brown
and beige carpet in the middle of the sanded and sealed
floorboards seemed new or newish.

'I'll get the sherry,' said Verna. 'It's in the kitchen.' She
returned moments later with a tray and two glasses.

'Christopher doesn't drink,' she explained as she
placed the tray next to a flowerless African violet on the
coffee table.

I noticed she drank her sherry quickly and for a while
she chatted about her work with the disabled. We were on
to our second sherry when she talked of other things.

'Poor Christopher has had a bad time lately. What with his skin condition and having a crush on that district nurse. She was sympathetic, you see, gave him time, listened to him. That's why we've allowed him to have the puppy. My husband doesn't like dogs but even he has a soft spot for Janey.'

'What about when Christopher goes back to college, who will look after the dog?'

Verna sighed. 'I really don't think he will go back. He's talking about accountancy or hotel management. Even my husband doesn't seem to be too disappointed. He thinks the Church of England is on its last legs. Mind you, he's been very depressed lately. I think Christopher has worried him.'

'In what way?'

'Oh, his lack of friends; well, our lack of friends really. The only people I seem to meet are elderly ladies. Younger women seem to think that because I'm the vicar's wife I'm hardly a person at all. I have to be so proper. I'd love to wear red mini-skirts and six-inch heels but it isn't done, is it?'

'I do understand,' I said. 'I lived with a police inspector for a while. Friends suddenly become careful about what they say. There are so many things they just don't mention any more: car tax, MOTs, TV licence, income tax, speeding, drinking, even finding a pound coin in the street. Somehow they become cagey and defensive. After a while I found I could only be at ease with other police girlfriends and wives.'

Verna smiled. 'At least you didn't have to pretend to be religious.'

Christopher returned then and soon we could hear sounds of cooking and the smell of curry began to drift towards us.

The meal was so good I could see that a vicar's life was not for Christopher. He also seemed shy but normal, with a dry sense of humour. Mr Collicot senior was, it seems, at a church meeting and was out on some mission most evenings. The dessert was spotted dick with custard but I could only manage half and excused myself from the table while Christopher was making coffee.

Upstairs I found the bathroom easily enough and then, feeling as nervous as a novice burglar, I gave a quick glance behind each door. Christopher's bedroom held no obvious dark secrets. No Hitler posters, no gun books, no martial arts equipment. There was a pair of weights but I didn't think that constituted a murderous nature. I was just closing the door when Janey came happily sniffing round my ankles. Then she started to bark and I made a hasty retreat downstairs with her close on my heels.

'You will come again, won't you, Kate? I have enjoyed having you,' said Verna.

Christopher walked with me along the drive to the front gate.

'Please,' he said earnestly, 'if you have any news about Vanessa let me know and if you see her give her this.' He handed me a thick envelope. As I hesitated he said, 'Please. I know I'm ugly and younger than she is but I'd look after her. It's not so ridiculous, is it? I can't help it. I think she is the most wonderful person in the world. You will give her the letter, won't you?'

'I'll try my very best,' I said. 'But I don't know when the police will allow me to see her. Maybe not until he's caught.'

'Have the police got any clues?' he asked. 'Have you?'

'They are working very hard,' I said. 'But a mere investigator like me doesn't get any police help.'

He nodded. 'I understand.'

As I opened the heavy metal front gate I asked, 'That black van of your mother's, do you ever drive it?'

'Yes, sometimes.'

'Have you ever parked in Percival Road watching Vanessa's house?'

He stared at me for a moment in a mixture of embarrassment and fear. 'Just the once,' he said. 'That's the truth. I just wanted to make sure she was all right. Maybe just catch a glimpse of her.'

'God's honour?'

'God's honour,' he repeated, and I believed him.

TWENTY-ONE

THE NEXT MORNING I'd just staggered from a far too hot bath feeling a bit light-headed when Hubert phoned.

'You're back,' he said.

'I was only helping at the fête. I had supper with the vicar's wife.'

'Coming in today?'

'Should be in later on this morning.'

'Good. I've got some news.'

'So have I.'

Even as I spoke Hubert had put down the phone. What happened to pleasantries? I wondered.

When I did arrive at Humberstones the receptionist met me on the stairs. 'He's not in, dear. He's been called out again. Twice in the night and just a few minutes ago. He's getting a bit worried about space.'

'Thanks for letting me know,' I said as I continued up the stairs.

'Come and have a coffee with us,' Daphne Gittens called after me. 'We don't see much of you.'

It seemed churlish to refuse so I followed her down to the back room behind the main office.

At a trestle table, arranging flowers in a vase, sat a thin spotty girl with half her head shaved.

'This is Yvonne,' explained Daphne. 'She's come to give us a hand with the laying out. Very ambitious is Yvonne—wants to own her own business in a few years.'

Yvonne smiled crookedly and said, 'Hi.'

'What sort of business?' I asked.

She looked at me pityingly and I realised it had been a stupid question.

'Funeral directing, of course, and embalming.'

'Of course,' I muttered awkwardly.

'Have you heard the news?' she asked.

'No. What news?'

'Lots of excitement here last night. Police everywhere. Sirens, the lot. It was better than the tele—'

'Don't romanticise, Yvonne,' interrupted Daphne. 'It's very serious. There's a girl's life in danger and he seems to have got away.'

'What's happened?' I asked, trying to stay calm. 'What's been going on?'

'Ooh! You've gone all pale,' said Yvonne in obvious delight.

'Sit down, Kate. I'll get you a cup of coffee,' said Daphne.

'No, please don't worry,' I said. 'Just tell me.'

Daphne gave a warning look to Yvonne to be quiet and the girl's lips pursed in an effort to keep them stilled.

'Last night, dear,' she began as she sat down, 'last night that poor girl was taken from a house in Percival Road. Kidnapped she was. And the police were supposed to be guarding her. Mind you, he was clever. He set up a diversion. A fire in the house opposite. While all that was going on, he got in and took her.'

'But I thought she was at a secret hideout with a woman police constable,' I said, the shock giving way to anger. 'How the hell could they let this happen?'

'It seems she wanted to come home and the police thought a constable keeping an eye on the house from outside would be enough.'

'Didn't anyone see anything? Surely she can't have just disappeared?'

'No dear. She's gone. Not a trace at the moment, but of course the police are out in force combing the area.'

'And the man?'

'No one saw him, at least I don't think so. Invisible, that's what he was—the invisible man.'

'Exciting, in'it?' giggled Yvonne, unable to keep quiet any longer.

'Not for my client,' I said. 'Not for her.'

'You've heard,' said Hubert when he saw me later staring out of my office window.

'I've heard,' I said glumly, not looking up. Somehow I felt if I stared long enough at the High Street it would yield up clues like the litter and dust caught by the wind that sailed forwards and then stopped, settled and then moved forwards again . . .

'What are you going to do?'

'I don't know, Hubert. I wish I did. What the hell are the police up to? I know she wanted to go home but surely they could have persuaded her.'

'Perhaps,' said Hubert slowly, 'they were trying to lure him there. Vanessa must have agreed to it, after all. I don't suppose they dragged her home kicking and screaming.'

I looked Hubert straight in the eye, 'Sometimes, Hubert, you make me sick. You can be so rational and calm and—right. It can be very irritating, you know.'

Hubert shrugged and smiled in unconcealed delight. 'You won't find her sitting on your backside,' was his only reply.

I was quite surprised at his tone and I must have shown it because Hubert smiled again, but this time sheepishly, sat down, and said, 'Come on, Kate, it's not like you to get downhearted. You've usually got a scheme or two lurking up your sleeve, and anyway you've only got two choices, haven't you?'

'Which are?'

He tutted at that, and raised an eyebrow like a junior school headmaster whose star reader had just got a word wrong. 'Go and look for her,' he said, 'or leave it to the police.'

'I don't want to admit defeat. I want to be the one to find her. But she could be anywhere. He could have killed her by now.'

'Unlikely,' muttered Hubert. 'His mission was to get her. Now he's got her he might relax and not be so vigilant.'

'The invisible man,' I mumbled, thinking aloud. 'Just like Yvonne said.'

Hubert obviously didn't hear because he said nothing but my defeatism began to lift. Vanessa probably knew him before. Maybe I'd met him at some time. It was only that I hadn't recognised him because either he was so ordinary or because I was just too blind to see.

'Hubert,' I said triumphantly as I stood up and picked up my coat, 'the brain's back in gear. The backside is ready for take-off. I'm going to rescue my client.'

He scowled. 'You're changeable,' he said. 'Now don't get over-confident and start taking risks. If you left it to the police it wouldn't do you any harm—'

'Oh yes it would,' I interrupted. 'My professional pride would be damaged.'

'Be more than that if you get blasted with a shotgun,' he said dourly. 'And anyway what profession are you talking about?'

'Every day I'm gaining experience, Hubert. Learning a bit more about human nature, a bit more about detecting skills. One day perhaps the police will seek help from me.'

'And I might inherit a shoe factory,' said Hubert.

Just as I was leaving he patted me on the shoulder. 'Talking of shoes. Don't forget that when actors want really to get to know a character they get the walk right first. Must mean something.'

'It must mean something,' I mumbled quietly to myself. And then I knew. 'Hubert, you are a genius!' I enthused, giving him a peck on the cheek and rushing out before he had time to ask me what I was up to.

I drove to Percival Road, stopped a few doors down from number thirty-six and sat in the car wondering why I had been so optimistic, especially when I saw the fire damage to the house opposite. I even smelt, or thought I did, the acrid smell of burnt furniture.

A uniformed police constable now stood guard outside Vanessa's house and inside I could see signs of activity, the movement of curtains, quick glimpses of masculine heads. It seemed strange to me that May Brigstock's death had caused hardly a ripple in the annals of crime. Paul Oakby's demise more so, but that had been real drama with TV cameras, extensive house-to-house enquiries and then—the lull. Now Vanessa had been kidnapped police activity seemed at an all-time high. Was this because there was still hope of saving her or because the police were embarrassed that they still hadn't caught the man responsible?

I must have sat a little too long because the policeman began to watch me intently. I knew that soon he'd come over and ask me what I was doing. So I pre-empted him, walked over to look him in the eye and said confidently, 'DS Roade wanted to have a word with me, Officer. Would you tell him I'm here—Kate Kinsella.'

'I'm not a messenger boy,' he said curtly. 'I'll let you in, but you'll have to be frisked first.'

I gave him a quick careful look. He was good-looking, young, quite presentable. 'I'm all yours,' I said, lifting my arms. 'You can take your time.'

The frisking he gave me must have been the quickest ever. My weak little joke had obviously scared him.

'Right. You can go in now.'

'Thank you so much, Officer. Do I get the same on the way out?'

His answering look said, not if I can help it, and he turned back to continue his street vigil.

Vanessa's house had obviously become some sort of operations HQ. I was surprised to see that Scene of Crime officers were still busy with rubber gloves on and large rolls of Sellotape at the ready. DS Roade and Inspector Hook stood around trying to look busy but instead managed to look a little lost.

'I'm sorry to interrupt but I wondered if there was any news yet?'

'Does it look like it?' answered Hook angrily, but with no surprise at seeing me. 'Would we be hanging around here if there was?'

I ignored his bad temper to ask how exactly HE got in.

'There was no sign of a forced entry. We think he may have had a key. It seems he took her out by the back door and along the alleyway behind the garden shed.'

'What about suspects?' I asked.

'What about suspects?'

'Well, I imagine you have several.'

'You imagine that, do you?'

'Yes, I thought maybe—'

'You did, did you?' he interrupted.

I felt myself become uncomfortable. I wasn't flavour of the month, that was certain and I wasn't quite sure how to tackle his aggressiveness. I glanced at Roade, trying to look helpless and mystified at the same time, but just as he opened his mouth one of the Scene of Crime officers came out of a cranny to say, 'We've finished now. We'll be off.'

'Took long enough. Let's hope you've got some good stuff for us,' said Hook.

I felt relieved his irritability wasn't just confined to me. He was sharing it around.

'Roade. Take Miss Kinsella for a walk somewhere. Get yourself something to eat and then continue with house-to-house enquiries. And for Christ's sake come up with something.'

'Come on,' muttered Roade, taking my arm. 'Let's go while we've got the chance.'

Roade continued holding my arm as we walked along Percival Road.

'Where to?' I asked.

'Any bloody where that'll serve me a fry-up. I'm starving.'

The Happy Sausage Café off the High Street provided just what Roade needed: two eggs, bacon, one obscenely large sausage, fried tomatoes, fried bread and strong dark tea. I ordered toast and tea and watched, with a tinge of jealousy, as Roade ate hungrily.

As an eating place the Happy Sausage offered clean Formica tables, unlimited tomato and brown sauce, and it was empty save for a tramp, two members of staff and a man in a leather jacket who looked as if he'd just parked his lorry.

'This is good. Really good,' said Roade as he bit into the crunchy fried bread and a little of the grease ran down his chin to be wiped away with the back of his hand.

'Have you got any leads?' I asked as he finished his last mouthful.

'I wish we had. Hook's been doing all the worrying, while O'Conner sits at the station doing sod all and giving Hook a hard time. And that means I get all the flak.'

'Tissot isn't a suspect?'

'At home again with the wife and kids. No reason to snatch her, was there? She was all his anyway.'

'And the ex-husband?'

'Out of the country selling computers.'

'And Sean?'

'In hospital having his appendix out. You can't get a more cast-iron alibi than that, can you?'

I sighed. 'What about the door-to-door enquiries?'

'No joy there either.'

'So what happens next? We can't just let her die. She's got to be somewhere.'

'We?' asked Roade.

'The police of course. He has killed twice. I'm just hoping he hasn't . . . well, hurt her—'

'It's on the cards, naturally,' interrupted Roade. 'We'll have to find her quickly.'

Roade avoided my eyes. He knew we were dealing with a madman. A man at the end of his psychological tether. A man with a shotgun who, it seemed, had been waiting for some time for this opportunity.

'Could you tell me why they took Vanessa back to her own house? Hook promised her protection. It seems very callous in the circumstances.'

Roade had the decency to look ashamed. 'That was a real cock-up,' he admitted. 'That was O'Conner's bright idea. He thought it might make our man attempt to see her.'

'Take her, don't you mean?'

'No, he thought with a man posted outside and Vanessa locked well in she would be safe. And she was desperate to get home. She insisted. Now they think HE may have managed to hide in the garden shed and then when the coast was clear to get in the house.'

'How, for God's sake?'

Roade blinked and looked away, embarrassed. 'If you must know the PC on duty had to go for a pee. He came back to find there was a fire and pandemonium broke out. It was only later when they couldn't get any answer from the house that they realised Vanessa had been taken.'

I couldn't blame Roade for that. In fact I was feeling increasingly sorry for him.

'What does HE hope to gain?' I murmured, thinking aloud.

'Who knows with a nutter?' said Roade. 'It's beyond me. I suppose it depends if he's obsessed with her or wants revenge for something. If he's obsessed she's got a chance of living—if she plays her cards right. She's got to talk to give herself time. If she starts screaming and tries to make a run for it ... well that's it.'

'DS Roade, you have hidden depths,' I said in admiration.

Roade turned his away in another bout of embarrassment but he recovered quickly to say, 'So has this bloke. That's what's stopping us finding him. A dark horse, a sleeping villain. But we'll get him in the end.'

'Just as long as we're in time to save Vanessa.'

'Yeah. Yeah,' said Roade. 'I've got to go now.'

'Just one thing before you go ...'

Roade stood up now, his stomach full, raring to be out and back on the hunt.

'Yes?'

'Colin Tiffield?'

'What about him?'

'You've seen him?'

'Of course. Our first choice. A nasty creep but he got sorted out.'

'How do you mean?'

'In prison.'

'Prison?'

'Yeah. Didn't you know?'

'No, I didn't.'

'He got ten years for raping a twelve-year-old. That's how he lost his leg. Someone threw him over a prison balcony. He was in a coma for three weeks. Didn't do his full term because of his injuries. The little bastard is even trying to claim compensation from the prison authorities for injuries sustained.'

'But he's not capable of doing that.'

'No, but Vanessa's sister has hired a brief. She's doing all the organising.'

'Vanessa didn't tell me. Why didn't she tell me?'

'It seems she didn't know. Her sister didn't mention her existence and unless she saw it in the papers how was she going to know?'

As Roade moved towards the till that stood near the door of the Happy Sausage, I asked, 'What time did Vanessa . . . get taken?'

'No one's at all sure. The fire started about eight thirty but we didn't find she was missing until ten.'

'Thank you,' I said.

That most certainly let young Christopher off the hook. He had been with me at the time the fire started.

Not that he'd been much of a suspect anyway, I thought dejectedly.

'See you then, Kate,' said Roade cheerfully as he paid the bill, insisting on paying for my tea and toast as well. 'Make sure you stay well out of this, won't you? You'll only make things worse if you interfere.' Then he added shyly, 'You can call me Rob if you like.'

'Gee thanks, Rob.'

I watched him stride purposefully away on his mission and I felt a tinge of envy that he had the comfort of someone telling him exactly what to do.

Walking seemed to be therapeutic because I managed to make two decisions. One was I was going to catch him, the other was I was going to save Vanessa. And, as if it might do some good, I kept saying to myself, just hang on, Vanessa. Just hang on!

TWENTY-TWO

I WALKED slowly back to Percival Road and sat for a while in my car. I couldn't go charging off to Derbyshire suggesting to an ex-con that his injuries were fake. Nor would that necessarily find Vanessa. He couldn't risk keeping her in the house because of Sheila, or could he? Did she know what was going on or did she deliberately turn a blind eye?

As I sat there a woman came out of the burnt house. I waited until she drew alongside me and then wound down the window. She was young and she'd been crying.

'Excuse me,' I said.

'You from the press?'

I shook my head. 'I'm an investigator.'

'Fire insurance?'

'No, not exactly. I just wondered if you could tell me what happened last night.'

She stared at me for a moment, her pale grey eyes still showing worry and shock. 'We're lucky to be alive. If the baby hadn't been crying and been with me downstairs we would never have got out. Our front room is gutted but the upstairs is okay. We were just lucky, very lucky. If a passer-by hadn't banged on my window to tell us the hall was on fire... Well, as it was... we managed to get out of the window.'

'Passer-by?'

'Yes, a woman. She definitely saved us.'

'How was the fire started?'

She shuddered slightly. 'A lighted rag in a bottle of petrol put through the letter-box, so the fireman said. Who would do such a thing?'

'And you didn't see or hear anything?'

Shaking her head she said, 'No. That's what is so scary. We didn't hear a thing.'

HUBERT MET ME in the hallway.

'I've got jam doughnuts,' he said, shaking a paper bag in front of my eyes, 'to cheer you up. They only need a cup of coffee to wash them down.'

'Come up then, but I haven't got much time. I'm going to Derbyshire.'

Once in my office Hubert tried to persuade me to wait until tomorrow.

'I'm free all day. I'll buy you lunch.'

'Hubert, you can't buy me for mere chicken and chips in a basket.'

'Pity,' said Hubert with one of his half smiles.

'I'm going to keep watch on Maple Cottage. I'm taking my camera and with any luck I'll get a photograph of Colin Tiffield doing things he's not supposed to be capable of. He might even lead me to Vanessa.'

As I mentioned Vanessa I felt depression hit me like a lead weight to the chest. He'd already killed her. He'd planned it long enough and now he'd risked his freedom to have his revenge. Revenge for what, though? After all she wasn't responsible for him going to prison. And it seemed that he had professed love for her. And why had no one seen him hanging around? Even if he had walked well with his artificial leg he would still have been stiff-legged and walked with a slight limp. Noticeable enough even for a busier place than Longborough.

'Is it wise,' Hubert asked, 'to go there on your own? You should have more sense.'

'I only plan to watch the house, Hubert. I'm not planning to do anything foolhardy but Vanessa could be still alive, shut up somewhere in the dark, terrified.'

'Of course she's alive,' said Hubert. 'You've got to believe that. Even so, it won't help her if you get hurt.'

'I'll be as careful as an elderly nun at Matins.'

'Wish I could believe that,' he said.

'Tell you what. How about if I leave the heroics till you are with me?'

Hubert frowned. 'I don't like the sound of that either. The police are trained to be heroes, we're not.'

'You're never satisfied, Hubert.'

He didn't answer and I made coffee and ate my doughnut while Hubert sulked.

'Ring me if you get into bother,' were his last words as he left my office, his doughnut and coffee left untouched.

I packed my instamatic polaroid into my shoulder bag, made a flask of coffee, sought out some biscuits and, as a final business-like token, I put on a scarf, gloves and a pair of boots.

Driving away from Longborough I was given a bit of a jolt by the sight of search parties wending their way through fields towards barns and outhouses. Silhouetted against the greyish skyline they looked like stick men from a Lowry painting. A bit further on I passed another group. Led by a few uniformed police officers, the bulk of the numbers were made up of villagers who looked as if they were out on an afternoon ramble and occasionally thrust walking sticks into the roadside bushes. They walked two abreast and I had to slow down to pass them. Somehow those thrusts into the hedgerows depressed me. It was as if they were convinced that all they would touch was something that would not be disturbed by a stick. Like a body.

Halfway to Bonsall, spring stepped back into winter. The sky grew dark and huge snowflakes fell relentlessly. My windscreen wipers hardly coped and I had to drop speed and turn off the car radio so that I could concentrate better. Soon the roads became slushy and the soft whishing noise became irritating. At that moment as I checked in the rear mirror I realised the noise I heard was not just snow on tyres but the sound of breathing and there in the mirror was a face. A man's face. The wheel juddered in my hand and the car skidded as I slammed down on both clutch and brakes. As the car finally stopped I was aware of my heart thumping in my chest and an 'Oh God!' that croaked from a dry throat.

'Sorry, Kate,' said Christopher Collicot. 'I didn't mean to frighten you.'

I still couldn't speak properly. I was too angry.

'You stupid...boy,' I managed to say. 'You could have killed us both. What the hell are you playing at?'

'I didn't think you'd be that frightened,' he said. 'I thought you were tough.'

'I am tough,' I said, 'and I'll clock you one in a minute to prove it.'

Christopher giggled nervously. 'I knew if I asked you wouldn't let me come. I heard about Vanessa and thought you might be going to look for her. I was coming to Humberstones to see you, and the car was there, the door was open so I slipped in under the blanket on the back seat. I thought I could be of some use...'

'The police are looking for her,' I interrupted. '*You* would have been more help on the search party.'

'Kate, I really am sorry. But I want to find her desperately.'

'So do I. And so do the police.'

I started the car, reasoning that even though I didn't want him with me I couldn't just abandon him at the side of an isolated road in the snow.

As I drove the steady rhythm of the wipers and the silent drift of snowflakes against the windows seemed to calm me. Perhaps Christopher could be of some use. Maybe we could get into Maple Cottage. Exactly how I hadn't worked out yet or what to do once we had, but even so it was worth a try.

I found the road to Maple Cottage quite easily. I was tempted to park the car at the bottom of the hill and walk from there, so that we could have a snoop round first, but the snow would have soaked us through and Christopher was already looking pinched and cold.

At the top of the hill I parked the car in front of bushes and trees just at the side of the driveway. No one could enter or leave without us seeing them because Maple Cottage was the end of the road. Stoned-walled fields, white with snow, were the only sight for miles around.

We sat for some time, drank coffee and ate biscuits. Christopher had to sit beside me in the passenger seat to share the blanket but even so we soon felt chilled. I'd just decided dying of hypothermia was an uncomfortable way to go when we heard a car start up.

I put my head on to Christopher's lap just after I caught a glimpse of the red of the car.

'Who was in it? What make?' I asked when I heard it go safely past.

'Red Golf,' said Christopher, 'newish. I only saw one in the car. A woman driver, I think; the snow was a bit too thick for me to see properly.'

We waited a while longer and then, because I wanted to prove to Christopher how decisive and tough I could be and because I was perished with cold, I said, 'Okay, Christopher, this is it. We're going in.' Then, as that sounded a bit exciting, I added, 'Not like the SAS, though; we're going in quietly, having a look round and then coming out. The man inside could well have a shot-gun at the ready and I don't want to be for ever known as the private investigator who got the vicar's son shot.'

'You are funny,' said Christopher. 'I was a boy scout, you know.'

'Well, let's hope you know more than dib, dib, dib, and how to tie a reef knot.'

'I can get through small windows and pick a lock and I know a bit of karate.'

'Which bit?' I asked, unconvinced.

He didn't answer and after that exchange I knew that we couldn't delay any longer, no matter how scared I felt.

We approached the house through the trees and bushes. The ground was wet and slushy with snow and even though I was wearing boots it splashed above the tops. Keeping to the side of the house well away from the still, dark windows I signalled to Christopher that I was going to creep under the window-sills and see if I could see anyone.

The first room was dark and empty. I crouched my way along to the second window and gingerly raised my head. Although this room was equally dark I could still see HIM slumped in an armchair, asleep. At first I didn't notice. But then his legs caught my eye. One trouser leg was empty. He wasn't wearing his artificial leg.

Creeping back to Christopher I whispered, 'It's okay, he's asleep. Let's go round the back and see if we can get in.'

Stealthily we walked to the back of the cottage. The kitchen door was firmly locked and even though Christopher insisted on trying out his all-purpose penknife it made no difference.

'I expect it's bolted from the inside,' I said. 'We'll have to try something else.'

We stared at the back of the house for some time. The kitchen windows were tight shut; all that was open was a small window on the second floor, probably a bathroom. Christopher, though, continued to stare upwards with the look of a man who has seen a revelation.

'Don't even think it, Christopher,' I said. 'You're slim but not that slim.'

'All I need is a ladder,' he said, still looking upwards and ignoring the snow that fell in great wet flakes on to his face.

Eventually, wet and increasingly cold, thinking perhaps it might be worth a try, I said reluctantly, 'Well, we could look for a ladder, I suppose.'

The garden shed only boasted a stepladder, a lawnmower, a few garden tools and two Calor gas containers. We were luckier with the barn-cum-garage at the side of the house. Hung on the wall was an extending ladder. And in the spacious interior, another car, a dark navy estate.

Carrying the ladder round to the back did at least warm us up. I stood at the bottom of the ladder, a foot well planted on the first rung while Christopher bravely began his boy scout ladder-climbing exercise.

By the time he got to the top I had to look away. I'm terrified of heights and that includes watching other people climb. Curiosity got the better of me, however, and I looked up to see Christopher manage to open the window wider and start easing his body through. He's doing it, I thought. And then he stopped. I heard him shout in a strangled fashion, 'I'm stuck,' and after a few moments when nothing happened he resorted to 'Help!'

I couldn't move. 'Push yourself,' I shouted, not caring if the one-legged man indoors woke. I would take my chance with a shotgun rather than attempt to climb the ladder.

'Help me,' cried out Christopher again.

I looked up and felt sick. I took hold of the sides of the ladder and lifted one foot upwards. Just one step at a time. Don't look down, I told myself.

'Help, please help me.'

His voice seemed far away and disembodied and fluttered in the air like the snow.

And I still couldn't move.

TWENTY-THREE

CHRISTOPHER STOPPED shouting for help and had gone very quiet and still.

I started climbing slowly. On the fourth rung I stopped and started to make myself angry. 'Stupid stowaway—boy scout indeed—I'll . . .' It didn't work, anger couldn't overcome the fear. I kept on going slowly, fifth rung, sixth rung, saying to myself, just look up and you'll be fine but the snow half blinded me and I began to tremble.

Tightly holding the sides of the ladder I shouted up, 'I'm not going to make it, Christopher. If you want to see Vanessa again you'll just have to get through that window.'

I wondered at first if he'd heard, then his feet began to move and I could see he was trying, really trying.

'You can do it,' I called out.

And he did. I saw his legs inching through the window painfully slowly and then with a thump he disappeared.

Gazing upward I whispered, 'Thank you, Lord,' and began moving back down the ladder. Once I was on the ground I felt ecstatic. So much so that I forgot for a moment there was a probable murderer inside the house. The main man, faking brain damage to get compensation and being perfectly able to walk with one artificial leg. Douglas Bader had after all been able to fly a plane without benefit of any legs. Even now, I thought, Colin Tiffield could be strapping on that leg to come after us with a shotgun. Because surely he would have heard something, even if it was only the thump of Christopher falling to the floor.

With some difficulty I lowered the ladder and began dragging it back to the barn at the side of the house. There was still no sign of Christopher. Somehow I managed to get the ladder back in place and then I crept round to the front of the house and peeped through the window. Colin Tiffield slept on. At least he could have been asleep or dead. It was too dark for me to see the rise and fall of his chest, but he looked asleep.

I stood then under the porch with the sinister ivy overhead and waited. Eventually I heard movement, the sound of footsteps coming down the stairs, normal footsteps.

The door opened with a slight creak and there stood Christopher, pale, dishevelled and holding his wrist.

'I think it's broken,' he said, 'and I've been sick.'

'Sh...sh...' I said and then added in a whisper, 'he's still asleep. We'll go upstairs and I'll look at your wrist.'

Upstairs in the bathroom I examined Christopher's right wrist. It certainly looked broken: it was already beginning to swell, he could hardly move a finger and there was some deformity.

'I think it may well be broken, Christopher,' I said.

'And my chest is bruised,' he announced as he gingerly lifted his sweater and vest for me to see. Not only was he bruised but his window-entering had removed quite a lot of skin from his chest.

'You were very brave,' I said.

'You weren't,' he said reproachfully.

'We're all cowards sometimes, and I did try.'

He gazed at me for a moment as if about to argue but then his pallor increased and I had to sit him down quickly on the bathroom chair in case he decided to faint on me.

'You'll have to carry on being very brave,' I said. 'Till I get you to hospital anyway. Just wait here. I've got to check that Vanessa isn't anywhere in the house.'

He nodded, though I was sure it was only the mention of Vanessa that made him agree.

There was still no sound from below and I crept along the landing, opening the first door as quietly as I could. It was empty. The next small bedroom had an alarm clock by the bedside. I checked my watch. It showed the correct time. This room was definitely in use. The built-in cupboard was full of men's clothes. Sheila and Colin obviously slept apart. In the room next door which I assumed to be Sheila's I decided to have a closer look round. A half empty bottle of sleeping tablets sat on her bedside table. The name on the bottle said Colin Tiffield. At the bottom of a large wardrobe I found a photograph album. I flicked through it quickly. There were no photographs at all of Vanessa. Not one. Although Sheila in years gone by had looked very much like Vanessa and once or twice I had been unsure, the clothes and the age had been wrong.

The last door opened on to another empty room. Empty of a bed or furniture that is. All it contained was an oval mirror, ornately carved and fixed to the wall. The mirror Vanessa had painted. So this, I guessed, had been Vanessa's room. As I caught a glimpse of myself in that bare, sad room, I shuddered.

When I got back to the bathroom poor Christopher was crying with pain and shock.

'Come on,' I said, 'we're getting out of here.'

Holding his good arm I half lifted him from the chair and although he slumped at first, as he got used to being on his feet he was able to walk without help. Downstairs we had a choice of the front or back doors. I chose the back door, just in case Sheila returned and parked at the front.

Outside the snow had turned to sleet and once we were through the trees and bushes and the car was in sight I felt a great sense of relief. My car keys were still in my pocket but it was only when I'd got Christopher in the back seat and covered with the blanket that I realised I'd dropped my purse somewhere.

'I'll put that arm in a sling,' I said as I opened my first-aid kit, which I now always keep in the car since Hubert let it be known to me that it was a disgrace for a nurse not to have one. In it I kept a triangular bandage. With a few muttered curses because of lack of space I finally managed to support Christopher's arm in a sling. He smiled a little pathetically when I'd finished, but it *was* a smile. His improved spirits didn't last, though, when I told him I had to go back to the house.

'Please don't be long,' he begged, 'my arm's killing me.'

I found my purse easily enough in the barn by the ladder. All I have to do now is check out Colin Tiffield, I thought, but it also crossed my mind that anyone who sleeps through the noise we made is either very deaf or very dead . . .

Finding the right room was easy. Actually opening the door was a bit scary and I stood for a moment at the doorway before venturing inside.

Colin Tiffield was breathing, shallow, quiet breaths. I moved closer to his chair, noticing the empty trouser leg that almost touched the carpet. I stood watching him. Most people would have stirred because the draught from the open door was sharp as a knife. He didn't move. Was

he in a coma? I wondered. Feeling his hand first and being shocked by its coldness I moved my fingers round to
his wrist and felt his pulse—it was slow but regular. Too
slow. I shook him by the shoulder; there was no response.

I looked round the room. There was something missing. I had assumed when I didn't find it upstairs that it
would be in the room with him. I quickly searched the
rest of the ground floor and came back to him. His artificial leg wasn't in the house. I assumed Sheila had taken
it. I also assumed she had given him some sleeping tablets: that would account for the deep sleep. I felt one of
the radiators. It was cold. What on earth was she doing?
Taking away his leg, even doping him was, perhaps, her
way of controlling him. But leaving him uncovered in an
unheated house? Now that was definitely not mere control but attempted murder.

I rushed upstairs for a duvet and after I'd covered him
I rang for an ambulance.

'Your name please, dear?' asked a reassuring male
voice after I'd given him the patient's name and address.

I paused. 'Alison Dimwoody,' I improvised, feeling
that dim and woody was an apt description of my brain-
power at the moment.

'Right you are, Miss Dimwoody. You stay with the
patient. We'll be with you in no time.'

In the kitchen I found the central heating timer and
switched it on to constant and then I ran for the car.

'I'm cold,' said Christopher as I started the engine.
'You've been a long time.'

'He's even colder,' I said. 'I've sent for an ambulance.'

'For me?' he asked.

'No, I'm sorry, not for you. This would need too much explaining. You don't want to be charged with breaking and entering, do you? We'll find a hospital on the way back to Longborough.'

Christopher sighed but said nothing and I drove away, hoping that there actually was a hospital this side of Longborough. As we left Bonsall an ambulance passed us with blue lights flashing and I felt slightly guilty that I hadn't stayed, but at least Colin Tiffield would soon be warm and tucked up in bed. But in the meantime where was Sheila Wootten and, more importantly, where was Vanessa? Was she still alive?

I tried very hard to find a hospital for Christopher and I passed two but both had big 'THERE IS NO CASUALTY DEPARTMENT AT THIS HOSPITAL' notices. The nearest was Longborough General.

It was dark by the time we arrived in Longborough. Christopher had managed to sleep some of the way but as I parked in the General's car park he woke and said croakily, 'I must ring my parents. They'll be worried.'

'Where did you tell them you were going?'

'Out with the search party.'

'Do you think they will have phoned the police?'

'Probably. They would know the search would be abandoned when it got dark.'

'Let's get into casualty,' I said. 'I'll lie through my teeth. I'll say you fell behind the rest of the search party and slipped over and I found you in a ditch or something and brought you here.'

The casualty department was a haven of warmth but busy. I was disappointed to find I knew no nurses on duty and the glimpse I did catch of the casualty houseman told me he was a stranger too.

As Christopher gave his details to the receptionist I rang the vicarage from the public phone. The Reverend Collicot himself answered.

'I shall come immediately of course,' he said. 'I'm much obliged that you have been kind enough to take care of Christopher.'

I mumbled something about it being no trouble at all and felt my stomach churn with guilt pangs at telling such lies to a vicar. It was only later I realised the pangs were hunger.

I returned to sit with Christopher and explained that his father was on his way and knew the full story.

'You didn't tell him the truth?'

'Of course not. I told him a pack of lies but if he questions you seriously just say you can't remember. That way you won't feel so bad.'

'I couldn't feel worse.'

'Soon they'll have that arm in a plaster and you'll be home.'

'We didn't find Vanessa though, did we? I've failed her.'

'Of course you haven't. Really, Christopher, the boy scouts would be proud of you. You've been a real Trojan. And our trip has given me a new lead. Perhaps by tomorrow we will have found Vanessa.'

'Do you really think so?'

'Scouts' honour. Dib, dib, dib and all that.'

Christopher smiled weakly.

As I waved him goodbye I wondered if being such a good liar was a necessary character trait for all private investigators. Because I didn't have a lead and I was beginning to feel that the chances of finding Vanessa alive were very slim indeed. And where had Sheila gone off to and why had she tried to kill her beloved Colin? Was it because she wanted to save her sister? If so, she must know where Colin had put her.

Christopher's father was driving into the car park as I left. I kept my head down. I wasn't responsible for Christopher being in my car, I told myself. And I didn't want him to attempt that stupid window anyway.

Hubert greeted me with what I thought was his 'I've been worried about you expression' but it wasn't. It was his 'I've got bad news for you' look.

'You'd better come up to my flat,' he said. *That* boded ill. Especially when he told me to sit down, gave me a neat brandy and then stood nervously watching while I drank it.

'What's the matter, Hubert?' I asked as the first slug of fiery liquid hit my stomach.

'Bad news, Kate. I'm sorry.'

I knew then the expression on his face was the one he reserved for really grave news. Funereal graveness. I waited.

'Finish your drink,' he said.

I continued to watch his face as I drank the last of my brandy.

'I've just heard,' he said quietly, 'that a young woman's body has been found ten miles away. According to my sources it could be Vanessa.'

'No... it can't be... I don't believe it.' But I did and suddenly a knot formed in my stomach and the tears welled up like a geyser about to explode.

'There... there,' said Hubert, patting my back gently.

And that made me feel worse and then the tears dropped very conveniently into my empty brandy glass.

TWENTY-FOUR

HUBERT LET ME cry for a while, then he swapped my tear-smeared brandy glass for a fresh one and gave me what he called a 'good double'.

When I'd stopped sniffing and gulping he said, 'Do you want to talk about it?'

'No thank you, Hubert. You talk, I'll listen. What happened?'

'Well, it was some time this afternoon. The police began dragging the rivers and they came up with a body. The only info I've got is that it's a young woman. So far no one other than Vanessa has been reported missing locally.'

'Her sister's gone missing, but she's not young,' I said miserably. 'It does seem likely that it's Vanessa, doesn't it?'

Hubert nodded. 'You did your best.'

'My best isn't up to much, is it? I'm packing up the agency. I've had enough. Amateurs like me shouldn't be allowed out.'

'Now come on, Kate. The police couldn't protect her. Why should you do any better than the police?'

'Because she trusted me. Well, I think she did. I'll never know now, will I? Perhaps if I'd gone to Derbyshire sooner, not wasted my time with Dr Guilsborough...not—'

'If this body is Vanessa,' interrupted Hubert, 'you've still got a job to do. You've still got the murderer to find.'

'He's tucked up safe and warm in some hospital bed. And I suppose he's still acting dumb. I think Sheila thought she was doing the decent thing. Killing him gently. I expect she'd guessed for some time. Realised that what happened in the past wasn't Vanessa's fault and decided to play judge and jury. It wouldn't surprise me if she committed suicide now. She's got nothing left, has she?'

Hubert didn't answer as he poured himself a brandy and sat down on his splendid sofa.

'What exactly happened today, Kate? I'm confused. Is this Colin Tiffield dead or alive?'

'He was alive. I expect he'll be fine tomorrow when the sleeping tablets have worn off and his body's warmed up. I couldn't just leave him to die, could I?'

'Not your style at all,' said Hubert, smiling. 'But come on now, Kate, tell me all the interesting details and don't leave anything out.'

I told Hubert about Christopher nearly killing me with shock and about not being able to climb the ladder and then finding Colin semi-comatose. Hubert nodded and didn't say much.

All he said when I finished was, 'How about a sandwich or two and then you can get some sleep?'

'I can't think about sleep, Hubert,' I said. 'I've got to find...'

And then I remembered that it appeared it was too late to save Vanessa. I'd failed her.

I FELT A WEIGHT on my arm and heard Hubert say, 'Wake up, Kate. The police are here.'

I rubbed my eyes, trying to orientate myself to time and place. Hook and Roade stood there.

'Is this a dawn raid?' I asked turning myself on to my side, thinking I was in bed but finding myself perilously close to the edge of Hubert's sofa.

'Hardly,' said Hook. 'It's only eleven p.m.'

'Oh.'

'We hear you've been doing a bit of breaking and entering.'

'I wouldn't put it as strongly as that, Inspector. I did go in through the front door.'

'I don't want the details but if you did go in the front door who went through the bathroom window?'

'I couldn't divulge that, I'm afraid; it's against the PI's pledge.'

'What's that?'

'Thou shalt tell no one, least of all the police, of whosoever shall offer a helping hand, a bit of legwork or a word in the right direction. That name shall henceforth be sacrosanct and none shall prise the information forth with either bribes of money or threats or even torture.'

'Ha ha!' said Hook sarcastically.

'I thought that was pretty good for spur-of-the-moment stuff.'

'You might be quite good at finding willing helpers but you've had no more luck than us at finding Vanessa.'

'I thought...'

'You thought wrong, Miss Kinsella. The body we found is not that of Vanessa Wootten. She'd been in the water for at least two weeks and so far as we can tell she is younger than Vanessa and shorter. We haven't got a name yet but we're in touch with the Met and we're going through missing persons. No doubt in a day or two we'll have a name and hopefully her killer.'

'Thank you for telling me, Inspector.'

'I didn't come just to tell you that,' he said irritably. 'I came to warn you that next time you go house-breaking you'll be charged. We're only letting you off this time because you inadvertently saved a life. The hospital says he'll be fine tomorrow. In the meantime he's under police guard so don't attempt to visit him. He's been trying to speak but isn't able to do so. A miniature electronic keyboard is being delivered so that we can interview him. That is if he can understand our questions, let alone tap out the answers.'

'And Sheila Wootten and Vanessa?'

'Just leave them to us, Miss Kinsella. In fact leave everything to us. It'll be safer in the long run.'

As they left Roade waved and said, 'Bye, Miss Dimwoody,' and Hook gave Hubert an up-and-down look as if to say, 'How the hell did you get through that bathroom window?'

Once they'd gone I gave vent to my excitement. 'She's still alive, Hubert! I know she is and I've got another opportunity to find her.'

'Don't get carried away, Kate. She could be dead anyway.'

'There's still a chance and that's what matters.'

'What *are* you planning?' asked Hubert, frowning.

'Just a little hospital visit, that's all.'

'All! You heard Hook, Tiffield is under guard. The police are hardly likely to let you get a look at the ward door, never mind have a bedside tête-à-tête.'

'Well, he supposedly can't speak, so I can't do much harm, can I?'

'Why go then?'

'Because he might be in danger simply because he does know where Vanessa is, and if that word machine has arrived he might, just might, be able to tell me.'

'I thought,' said Hubert looking perplexed, '*you* thought he was the kidnapper-cum-murderer. How is it that you're now trying to protect him?'

'It's really very simple, Hubert. I had a dream and that's sorted out a few problems I had with this case. You see, he's not the main man.'

Hubert sighed. 'Well, if you're relying on dreams I think I'd better come with you. You may as well go in style. When do you want to go?'

'About two thirty. I can pretend I'm the night nurse. Whoever is guarding him will be at a low ebb in the early hours. It will be easy, you'll see.'

'I've heard that before,' said Hubert. 'I'm going to bed.'

As he walked off towards his bedroom I called after him, 'Don't forget to set the alarm, Hubert. You wouldn't want to miss this, would you?'

'I'm seriously thinking,' said Hubert turning to fix me with a glum stare, 'of upping your rent.'

PLUMBRIDGE General Hospital glistened with melting snow. The car park was only a quarter full and Hubert's posh white car swished quietly into a convenient position near the main door.

'Now what?' asked Hubert.

I began removing my coat, two jumpers, scarf, gloves and then felt a slight shiver as I sat in just my blue uniform dress.

'Simple, Hubert. I bluff my way in saying . . . well. I'll think of something but if the night porter questions me I'll run my fingers through my hair and you can come in saying you're the undertaker.'

'I see. I couldn't just rush in saying I was MI5.'

'No, Hubert. You don't look like a man from MI5. You look like an undertaker.'

'Thanks,' replied Hubert in a hurt voice. 'Then what?'

'I don't know. You'll just have to improvise long enough for me to get past the porter.'

'How will you know which ward he's on?'

'I hadn't thought of that,' I said slowly. 'Well, I'll just have to ask, won't I?'

'You haven't thought this through, have you, Kate? You just intend to go blundering in . . .'

'Don't go on, Hubert. Bet you a fiver we do it.'

'I'm not a betting man,' said Hubert primly, 'but I'll definitely up your rent if this turns out to be one almighty cock-up.'

I walked slowly towards the main door. The night air was cold on my bare arms but I had to pretend to be enjoying it and at the door I made a great show of doing a bit of deep breathing and arm-stretching.

As I opened the door I acted as if I were reluctant to come inside.

'Wonderful night,' I said. 'I really needed some fresh air. I'm agency and I usually work days. It's so hard to keep awake when you get too warm, isn't it?'

'I'm a night bird myself,' said the porter, who was rotund with dark bags under his eyes.

He didn't try to stop me so I walked past him. As I approached the corridor I faltered.

'I am sorry,' I said, turning back, 'I think I'm lost. It's my first night. I know I'm on male medical. It's the ward they are keeping that man under guard—they needed extra staff because of all the police activity. Could you direct me? I came out another way.'

'It's confusing when you're new, dear. You want Nelson ward. Up the corridor, turn left, up the stairs, then it's second door on your right. It's got a sign—you can't miss it.'

'Thank you for being so helpful,' I said. 'This is one of the friendliest hospitals I've ever worked in.'

The night porter took that as a personal compliment and smiled delightedly.

I walked quickly but with showy confidence towards the ward. It's all in the walk, I thought, remembering Hubert's words. He was right, of course; he often is.

I met no one at the entrance to the ward and the right room was easy to find because a young uniformed police constable sat outside on a straight-back chair reading a book.

'Good book?' I asked as I approached.

He smiled. 'Terrible. It's about giant man-eating hedgehogs that pierce their victims all over with huge spines before chomping through them.'

'Should keep you awake,' I said. 'I've just been sent to take Mr Tiffield's temperature. Is that okay?'

'Fine. His sister turned up an hour ago, spent a few minutes with him. She seemed pleased with his progress when she left.'

'I didn't know he had a sister?'

'Nice woman. Grey-haired, walked with a stick. Night sister said she could see him as she'd had a long way to come and had only just heard he'd been admitted.'

He continued reading his book as I entered the room.

The overhead bedside light was on and Colin Tiffield was turned away from me, facing the curtained windows. I went round to the side of the bed and pulled back the sheet and blanket that half covered his face. There was no need to take his temperature. It would have been on a minus scale. His eyes were open and staring and the blue of his face matched the dark blue of my uniform. A thick line of bruising encircled his neck. He'd been strangled with a piece of rope or similar. What was used was purely academic for *she* was on the loose.

I had to think quickly. If I reported him dead I would not only have to stay but I might fall under suspicion myself.

'Sorry to disturb you, Mr Tiffield,' I said loudly. 'You go off to sleep now. No one will be troubling you again.'

I paused then to take a few deep breaths before I opened the door.

'That was quick,' said the constable.

'He's very peaceful,' I said. 'As warm as he'll ever be.'

'Oh, good. I'll soon be going to my nice warm bed. It's been a hell of a long night.'

'See you,' I said.

He nodded and his eyes dropped to read more about homicidal hedgehogs as I made a hasty exit.

Trying not to run and trying to remember the way back, I walked as quickly as I could. Eventually I got back to the main entrance and the night porter.

'You back again, dear?' he said with what I thought was a touch of suspicion in his voice.

'I felt faint,' I said. 'I'm pregnant you see, early days but I seem to need more fresh air than I did.'

'I understand, dear. You mind you don't get cold outside, though. Want to borrow my coat?'

'No thanks. I'll only be out in the cold a few minutes. I'll be fine.'

At that moment a phone rang and he turned his attention to the switchboard and I was out of the door as he did so.

Hubert was waiting with a resigned look on his face.

'Get out of here quickly, Hubert,' I said, 'and I mean like—now!'

'What have you done?' he asked as he drove off with only a marginal sense of urgency.

'Do drive a bit faster,' I urged as he joined the main road.

'Why?' he asked. 'Are we being followed?'

'Not yet.'

'Where to?'

That was a question I couldn't answer. It wouldn't be long before they found the body and circulated my description.

'Which way?' asked Hubert irritably as we came to a crossroads. 'And why?'

'Please, Hubert, just drive fast and keep to the side roads. I'll think of something.'

'You'd better,' said Hubert, looking in his rear mirror. 'We are being followed.'

TWENTY-FIVE

EVEN AS I turned my head to look behind, the blue light began to flash and the high-pitched siren began its screaming.

'This is it, Hubert,' I said.

'I could step on the gas,' said Hubert. 'What do you think?'

Before I had chance to reply the police car was past us and signalling for us to stop.

'Too late,' said Hubert as he slowly pulled into a lay-by. 'Just be polite to them, Kate.'

Hubert wound down the window as a thin young constable approached the car.

'Is this car yours, sir?' he asked.

'Yes, Officer,' said Hubert meekly.

'Do you have your driving licence and log book, sir?'

From the glove compartment Hubert produced them both. I was most impressed, not only because he had them in the car but impressed with Hubert's general demeanour. It was as if he was used to being stopped.

The constable scrutinised the documents very slowly. Finally he looked up and said, 'Nice car, sir. Pity about the rear offside brake light that's not working. And about the speeding. I'd like you to step out of the car and breathe into this bag, sir.'

Hubert didn't argue. He did just as he was told. After the constable had examined the filter of the breathalyser there was a little nodding and chat and Hubert was handed a piece of paper.

The constable's last words as he walked away were, 'Don't forget to get that brake light fixed, sir.'

We watched in silence as the police car drove away. I hardly dared believe our luck.

'What did he say?' I asked.

'Fixed penalty speeding fine for doing seventy in a forty mile an hour zone and a warning about the brake light. Nice chap, though.'

Somehow I now felt deflated. My adrenalin levels were obviously on the wane. What would have happened, I wonder, if Hubert had stepped on the gas . . . the gas! Of course. Why hadn't I realised the significance of the gas before? The Calor gas cylinders in Sheila Wootten's barn. Why would someone who had gas-fired central heating have Calor gas? Unless that person used it elsewhere. Like in a caravan.

Hubert had just started the engine and was looking at me questioningly.

'What would you do if you kidnapped a woman?' I asked.

Sighing, he switched off the engine. 'That sort of talk is a bit too much for me, Kate. It's not a matter I've given much thought to lately.'

'Come on, Hubert,' I cajoled. 'Think about it now.'

After a while he said, 'She wouldn't be willing, would she?'

'Of course not. It wouldn't be kidnapping then, would it?'

He smiled. 'Well in that case I'd have to tie her up, or drug her, bundle her in my car and . . .'

'Yes?'

'Take her somewhere safe.'

'Precisely, Hubert. Somewhere where she wasn't likely to be found.'

'Wouldn't this kidnapping business take a long time to plan?'

'I think something like this has been in the planning stage for a very long time.'

Hubert watched me as I put on my extra sweater and my scarf and changed into my boots. Even though the car was warm I had suddenly become shivery.

'Now perhaps you can tell me what happened in the hospital, Kate.'

'He was dead, Hubert. He'd had a visitor. The policeman guarding him thought she looked harmless.'

Hubert's mouth dropped open a little. 'But if he's dead surely it's all over. He must have left Vanessa somewhere...'

'It's not quite as simple as that, but I think she's in a caravan somewhere. There were Calor gas cylinders in Sheila Wootten's barn. All we have to do now is find that caravan.'

Hubert's eyebrows raised. 'You're an optimist. Round Longborough there are at least three caravan sites. You weren't thinking of going further afield, were you?'

'No, Hubert. I'm sure it will be local.'

'Oh good!' he said sarcastically.

As Hubert drove off in the direction of Longborough via the B roads he said, 'You do realise that the police could have easily made the same connection as you.'

'Yes, but we can't assume they'll go to the same places as us at the same time. Anyway it doesn't matter who finds her really, does it? Just as long as someone gets there in time.'

We'd been driving a few miles when I saw car lights in the wing mirror.

'Hubert, who's behind us?'

He glanced in his rear-view mirror. 'It's not a police car, Kate, so relax.'

'What sort of car is it?'

'I don't know. Maybe a Lada. I only know the quality end of the market.'

'Bear with me, Hubert. What colour is it?'

'It's dark red or black. It's difficult to tell. Would you like me to stop it and give it a full inspection?'

'Don't get riled. Only one more question. Who is driving?'

'Now you're getting silly, Kate. How would I know who's driving?'

'Male or female?'

Hubert looked into his mirror and the staring lights of the car behind. 'We'll have an accident if this carries on. Anyway I don't know. I can't be sure. It's too far behind. If it was my own father I couldn't tell.'

'What about your mother?'

'She couldn't drive. Can I concentrate on the road ahead now before we land up in a ditch?'

I stayed silent for a while. The Lada eventually turned off down a lane and soon the road signs told us Longborough was within ten miles. There was one big caravan site I knew of, holiday homes that opened in May and closed in October. Enclosed by fences and not easily accessible in the winter.

'We won't be able to get into Lakeview Holiday Park,' said Hubert as if he'd guessed what I was thinking. 'I think they have guard dogs patrolling.'

'Probably just a few "Guard Dogs Patrolling" signs up; it's cheaper than real dogs and it's bound to deter people.'

'Last time we were on one of these jaunts I was savaged by a dog. I haven't forgotten even if you have.'

'That was only a scratch, Hubert. This time we'll have no trouble with dogs. I'm sure of it.'

'Huh,' he muttered.

The road to Lakeview was narrow, tree-lined and so long and winding that we thought we had made a wrong turn. Until, that is, we came to the entrance. There at the wrought-iron gates were three police cars, lights blazing, and the sound of police dogs and the sight of as much police activity as Longborough could muster if the FA Cup Final was to be played there.

'Drive on, Hubert,' I said, putting my head between my knees so that hopefully I wouldn't be seen. I expected to be stopped but Hubert drove on slowly and nothing happened.

After a mile or so Hubert said, 'There's a small permanent caravan site the other side of Longborough and the other one is a gypsy site so it's not likely that Vanessa would be there, is it?'

'Try the permanent one then.'

Somehow the spark had left us both. Hubert drove silently, except to make the comment that he could do with a good breakfast. I debated with myself how long my bladder would last. And when we did find Vanessa would we be in time?

The permanent caravan site was well away from the town, a mere five or six homes arranged in a walled field. Three of them had their lights on although it was only just six a.m. and still dark and murky. As Hubert parked the car I said, 'You stay here, Hubert. I'll make a few enquiries. They might not open up if they see you.'

'I'm only the driver,' he said.

My enquiries didn't take long. At the first caravan I called on the door opened and an irate middle-aged woman in a dressing-gown said, 'Now what? I'm sick of this. Haven't we been disturbed enough? First we get the police in droves, now it's . . . well, what do you want?'

'I am sorry. I am a policewoman, I've been sent back to ask about any more caravan sites in the area.'

'Don't the police have maps? The lot that came before seemed to know where they were. They found us, didn't they?'

'I'll be in trouble with the Inspector if I don't come back with something.'

Her thin face softened a little. 'Look love, Longborough isn't that keen on caravan sites, especially permanent sites. They think it lowers the tone. There are only three proper sites. And of course those who keep their caravans in their fields or back gardens.'

My heart sank at the thought and I must have looked despondent because she said, 'I didn't mean to moan, love. You police are only doing your job. I just hope you find that poor girl. But as for caravans...mind you...I've just thought. There's a farm over by Little Charnford, two miles the other side. The farmer sometimes has a caravan to let. I was over there last summer doing a bit of pick your own strawberries and someone was renting it then.'

'Did you see them?'

'Oh yes, dear. It was a couple. He was in a bad way. Couldn't walk very well. Lord knows why they were there because it's only a field, there's no proper facilities. Perhaps she did a bit of farm work just during the summer.'

'Thank you so much,' I said. 'You may have just saved a life.'

'That's nice, dear. Glad to be of help.'

As I got back into the car Hubert said resignedly, 'Where to now, madam?'

'A mere few miles,' I said. 'A farm the other side of Little Charnford.'

'When this is over, Kate, you and I are going somewhere for a slap-up breakfast: eggs, bacon, sausage, mushrooms, fried bread—the lot.'

'No tomatoes or black pudding?'

'I could manage that.'

'If we find Vanessa—yes. If not I won't be able to eat.'

It began to snow again as we passed through the tiny hamlet of Little Charnford. It was easy enough to find the farm; it seemed to be the only one for miles. At first I couldn't see the caravan because it was in a field behind the main farm building. But as we drove past, there it was: old and a tired white with a thin blue stripe running along its side. Both the farm and the caravan seemed neglected and deserted. I'd hoped to find Sheila's red Golf but the only vehicles around were a Land-Rover and a tractor.

'Come on, Hubert, let's have a look round.'

'I expect the police have already done that.'

'Don't be so sure. We could get lucky.'

Hubert left the car reluctantly, pulling up the collar of his overcoat and then began searching in his coat pocket for something.

'Want a swig?' he said, showing me a small silver flask.

'Brandy?'

'Do you good.'

'It won't, Hubert, it just causes peripheral dilatation of the blood vessels.'

'Does that mean it will warm me up?'

'It will seem to but really...'

'I'll settle for that, Kate.'

I refused to drink any. I didn't want my wits dulled nor any of my brain's vital blood supply ending up in warm fingers. My brain needed all the help it could get.

There was still no sign of life in or around the farm and the caravan door was locked. On tiptoe I peered through the windows. It was empty. One Formica table with bench seats and cushions plus a window seat and a wall cupboard was all that space allowed. Disappointment welled inside me, until I saw it. Just a shimmer by one of the bench seats and then my breath on the windows made it disappear.

'We need a crowbar, Hubert, or a hammer. We have to get in.'

Hubert tramped back to the car and opened the boot. Moments later he came back, crowbar in hand. 'Right, stand back,' he said as he began to force the lock.

It took longer than I expected but with a final heave and a wrench the lock gave and we were in.

The caravan had the smell I expected of all caravans, Calor gas and plastic and a slight staleness. The silence and the emptiness were even more disappointing inside. Even the shimmering gold on the floor was not, as I expected, one of Vanessa's golden hoops, but a tiny piece of screwed-up gold foil. As I bent to pick it up I heard something. A groan or a sigh: I wasn't sure which, but something! Hubert heard it too. We looked round but there was nothing to see. The sound had stopped now but we searched in the shower compartment and the portaloo and in the one full-length cupboard. But all was still and silent. We waited, trying not to breathe too loudly lest we blocked the tiniest sound. Then after a while we heard a movement, just a shuffling sound but this time I knew where it was coming from. Quickly I lifted the bench seat lid up and there, knees drawn up to her chest, hands tied behind her back, mouth taped with Elastoplast, was Vanessa. Her eyelids flickered but didn't open. We both bent to lift her out and as we did so we failed to hear the movement behind us or see the face of the person who dug the gun into the small of my back. The voice, though, I recognised.

'Move and you're both dead,' said the voice.

TWENTY-SIX

HUBERT AND I seemed to stay in that undignified position for ages. The barrel of the gun pressed into my back was only half as painful as my full bladder. And far from my life flashing before me, the only thought that occupied my mind was I didn't want to wet myself.

'We can't stay like this, Sheila,' I said eventually, my voice sounding as if it were coming from my feet. 'Let us straighten up, please.'

'Lie on the floor then—you first.'

The gun barrel had gone from my back and Hubert was suddenly sprawled on the floor.

'You next.'

I was prodded and kicked, then I too lay on the floor.

'Put your hands behind your head where I can see them.'

Sheila's voice came out low and husky as if well practised in giving orders or in faking telephone calls.

We did as we were told and then lay without moving. I struggled to think back to all the films I'd ever seen. This was the point when someone always comes up with a merry quip or at least tries some sort of plea bargaining. The 'you'll never get away with it' scenario. But she had got away with it and somehow I doubted that she cared now if she lived or died. She had after all killed Colin. And the others.

I heard her stepping backwards and sensed she'd sat down. What now? Then Hubert began mumbling. He

was on the second line before I realised what he was saying—the Twenty-Third Psalm.

'I'll not want, he maketh me down to lie...'

Substitute he for she and lie for die, it was about right.
Not now, I wanted to say, it's not the right time, but then
I realised that it was.

'Be quiet,' said Sheila. 'I can't hear.'

At first I assumed she meant voices in her head, then I
realised there was the sound of footsteps outside. Oh
blessed cavalry, I thought, just in the nick...She was on
her feet then at the door; I could see her boots level with
my eyes.

'What's going on? Who's broken in? What the...?'
The male voice trailed off.

'Stand still,' shouted Sheila.

'Put that gun down,' said the man. 'Have you gone
mad?'

It was his last question. The blast rang out and I heard
one gurgled scream and a thump as he fell. I waited for
the barrage of shots at us. Please don't shoot me in the
back, I thought. Never mind my past life, it was my future I was worried about, I didn't want to be left alive and
paralysed.

In an agony of stillness we waited. Then I opened my
eyes. The boots were no longer by the door. She had
moved behind us. Hubert began mumbling again about
pastures green. That poor man outside wouldn't be seeing any more pastures, green or otherwise. He was, I
guessed, the farmer.

Vanessa groaned then. In my fear I had forgotten her.

'Let her out, Sheila. She doesn't deserve this, you
know. She didn't mean you any harm.'

'We'll be going together, her and I. I do love her, you
know. I always have. I had to tie her up and keep her

here. She tried to escape, you see. She always tried to escape. I should have told her the truth but I left it too late. Colin lied to me, you know. All along he lied. He told me the truth in the end, though. I taught him sign language and he was beginning to get some speech back and then he told me. I couldn't let him live after that, could I? Not after what I'd done.'

I didn't know what Sheila was talking about but at least she was talking which was supposed to be therapeutic for people with homicidal tendencies or was it suicidal tendencies? I couldn't think clearly anyway. My arm muscles had knotted now into painful spasm and that and a full bladder seemed to blot out any attempt at coherent thought.

It was then we heard the sound of cars arriving. It's all over. It's all over. The police. The cavalry. Death's dark vale retreating.

Sheila's boots were once more at the door. She swung it open with a soft sound of polymers clashing.

'Stay back!' she screamed. 'I'll shoot.' To prove it she fired.

Nothing happened. For a moment I imagined I'd heard those cars. Soon they'll be shouting through a megaphone and a mediator would talk Sheila out. Time passed and still nothing happened.

'Have they gone?' I asked.

'No.'

'Sheila, I have to go to the loo.'

'Wait.'

'I can't.'

Eventually she said, 'Crawl, then. Turn to your right and crawl. If you stand up before I say I'll shoot you.'

I crawled. Slowly and without removing my arms from behind my head. It wasn't far but it seemed a long way.

'Stop,' she said as I got to the door. 'Stand up.'

I stood up, painfully stiff.

'You can go in now.'

The bliss of moving my arms and relieving my bladder were such that I thought I'd never forget it—ever. Somehow the physical relief gave me new heart. I didn't want to die. I wasn't going to die. Somehow I had to do something.

'I'm coming out,' I called, in case she shot me in panic. As I crawled back to my place beside Hubert, for the first time I got a proper look at Sheila. She was wearing a man's black donkey jacket with leather patches at the shoulders, black jeans and mud-covered thick-soled black boots. Her hair she'd scraped back under a cloth cap. From a distance, even a short distance, she looked like a stocky middle-aged man. I managed to wink at Hubert. He winked back at me.

My euphoria was short-lived. Nothing had changed. But then I remembered the police outside. Perhaps they had sent for marksmen by now. It would soon be over.

'Sheila,' I said in a wheedling voice, 'please let Vanessa come on the floor with us. You can still keep her tied up but she must have terrible cramp by now. What difference can it make to you?'

She didn't answer at first, then she said, 'All right, get her out but just you. He's not to move.'

Pulling Vanessa out took all my strength. She blinked but then seemed to pass out. Her face seemed drained of all colour and just beneath her eyes were blue patches as if she'd been choking. I heaved her on to the floor and lay beside her for a moment, breathless. There must have been movement outside because Sheila moved towards the door.

'Come out with your hands up,' boomed a voice I didn't recognise.

I had to give the Longborough police zero out of ten for originality. Sheila wasn't impressed either. She raised the shotgun and took aim. In the seconds her attention was taken from us, Hubert's long arms reached out and with both hands around her ankles he had felled her. The shot rang out as the gun dropped from her hands and she toppled heavily backwards. Hubert sat on her legs and I made a grab for the gun. There was no moment of elation because from outside I heard the word 'Fire' and through the open door came what for a second I thought was a hand grenade. Then it exploded into a cloud of gas. Tear gas. I tried to crawl over to Vanessa to remove the plaster from her mouth but I was choking, crying and suffocating all at the same time. I got a vague impression that her face was going blue but then I couldn't see anything. The air around me turned black and it was as if I were in some deep swirling cavern going round and round and all the time gasping for air like a fish with a hook caught in its throat.

Then suddenly I was aware of being dragged along and bundled out into cold fresh air. My lungs felt as though they were bursting, my throat hurt and my eyes stung. Blue uniforms surrounded me and I tried to push them away. I wanted the whole sky full of fresh air.

'Come on, love. It's only oxygen. Take a few whiffs like a good girl.'

I breathed deeply as a mask was held to my face.

'That's better. You'll soon feel right as rain.'

I opened one sore eye to look at the ambulanceman. He smiled down at me and suddenly he seemed like the most attractive man in the world.

'How's Vanessa and Hubert?' I asked.

They were, it seemed, 'right as ninepence'. I looked round for them but couldn't see them.

'They're in the ambulance, love. Can you make it on your feet?'

'Yes, thanks. I'm feeling better now.'

Hubert sat upright in the back of the ambulance looking a strange puce colour but smiling. Vanessa lay having oxygen on a stretcher. Her eyes opened slightly as I said, 'Sorry I took so long to find you.'

She closed her eyes but I think she mumbled, 'That's all right.'

I HALF EXPECTED us to be VIPs at Longborough General but although Vanessa was whisked away to be examined, there had been a serious road traffic accident and Hubert and I had to sit in reception and wait. Being gassed by the police obviously didn't make us priority cases.

'You feeling okay, Kate?' asked Hubert, smiling happily.

'Never better.'

Hubert's near-death experience seemed to make him feel cheerful. In contrast I felt exhausted and depressed.

'Where are the police?' I asked. 'Keeping a low profile?'

'They'll be after us soon enough.'

'Did you see Sheila?' I asked.

'I certainly did. She was taken away by police car. I expect the police surgeon will take a look at her.'

We continued to wait and wait. A screaming child was brought in by anxious parents and that proved too much for Hubert.

'If we're both feeling fine now, why do we have to hang around here?'

I shrugged. 'Don't ask me, Hubert. I've never been tear gassed before.'

'We could just do a bunk, go and find that cooked breakfast I've been fancying for hours.'

I thought for a moment. I could almost smell fresh coffee and bacon. The choice between that and a cold stethoscope was an easy one.

'You're on,' I said, 'but the police could be waiting outside.'

'Do you know another way out, Kate?'

'Follow me. Try to look casual, though.'

The police had obviously driven Hubert's car to the hospital. One or two uniformed officers were standing around the car, either checking it for faults or admiring it. Hubert's wide American sedan was easily the most ostentatious in Longborough. We sneaked along the side of the hospital and stood outside.

'We could ring for a mini-cab from the phone box and go to the Happy Sausage,' I suggested.

'The Happy Sausage!' said Hubert incredulously. 'We're having breakfast at the Grand.'

The Grand Hotel provided us with their Grand Slam Breakfast. A similar breakfast to the Happy Sausage but on smart plates and with less grease. And with freshly squeezed orange juice, croissants and jugs and jugs of fresh ground coffee. The surroundings were of course a vast improvement and it was only when we were recovering from a day's worth of calories in the large shell-like chairs of the Grand's lounge that Hubert said, 'Are you going to explain this…adventure or do I have to guess?'

'I'll explain it as best I can, Hubert. Vanessa was fourteen when she suffered at the hands of Colin Tiffield. I think Sheila became very bitter then, blaming Vanessa for lying, for trying to spoil her life, for wrecking her chances of a marriage and a family, for "leading him on". Perhaps for a while she calmed down but then Colin got up to his old tricks again with a young girl. Instead of blaming Colin she blamed the girl and Vanessa of course. Then he went to prison and the "accident" happened. Bitterness festered in Sheila. She took to keeping tabs on Vanessa. Very cleverly of course...'

'Hang on,' said Hubert. 'Didn't she give a description of a man?'

'A very vague description, yes. But of course she assumed the man to be Colin Tiffield. You said to me once that the fear of being followed was contagious. You also said it was all in the walk.'

'Did I? I don't remember.'

'I still thought Tiffield was shamming his injuries but if a woman wants to look like a man it's her body language that she needs to change. And of course it is hard actually to see a person behind you in a car. All you really register is a general shape or something striking like flaming red hair. Sheila set out to be invisible; middle-aged women often complain of being invisible, and that's what she was. Not the invisible man, as Yvonne suggested, but the invisible *woman*. Even on the night of the fire no one could give a description of her and Vanessa hadn't, after all, seen her for several years. She sensed more than saw a person following her. I also doubt that Sheila actually did much following. The fear already implanted in Vanessa's mind was hard to shift.'

'That's all very well but what about the phone-calls?'

'Those, Hubert, were well practised. A telephone line always makes the voice seem deeper and she talked in a dull stylised monotone. Which was why Vanessa wasn't sure about the voice.'

Hubert gave me an old-fashioned look of the type that said 'I'm not totally convinced'.

'Tell me, then, why did she start killing people?'

'I can only guess at that, Hubert. Maybe she didn't feel Vanessa was suffering enough. Perhaps her beloved Colin wasn't making the progress she desperately hoped for. Killing May Brigstock was a prelude to killing her own sister. And of course she got away with it. The farm nearby held the answers but I concentrated far too much on Vanessa's men friends. I should have asked more questions in Little Charnford. Sheila had a connection with that farm and the village.'

'And the policeman's death?'

'I think Sheila arrived at the house planning to kill Vanessa, Paul Oakby was there and she panicked and killed him instead.'

'But why kill Colin? It seems he was beginning to improve.'

'Ah, Colin. I think he improved too much. He let it be known that not only had Vanessa not lied but Sheila finally recognised in him the evil that she perhaps knew subconsciously was there, but didn't want to admit to herself. No one, after all, likes to admit they love the unworthy. She had killed for a man who just wasn't worth it.'

'Well,' said Hubert thoughtfully. 'That's an awful lot of guesswork. Why on earth did she kidnap Vanessa and not kill her straight away?'

'That is puzzling me. Was she suddenly overcome with guilt or did Vanessa manage to talk her out of it? Perhaps some vestige of sisterly love still existed. I think she was contemplating both murder and suicide and then we came along and well . . . you were there.'

'Yes and what a cock-up. Wasn't like the films, was it? Hours of patient negotiations and requests for drinks and sandwiches. All we got was a gassing.'

'I think the Longborough police were a bit short on patience but then they didn't know we were already winning, did they?'

Hubert laughed. 'We did quite well really, didn't we? Teamwork, you see, that's what matters.'

'Indeed it does, Hubert,' I said, 'indeed it does.'

TWENTY-SEVEN

IT WAS THREE DAYS before we saw Vanessa again. Three days in which Hubert and I had to give long and detailed statements and listen to equally long lectures from Inspector Hook who called me a 'rank amateur' and a 'foolhardy girl'. I was grateful for the 'girl' but it was still difficult not to retaliate. Every time I opened my mouth Hubert kicked me on the ankle. Eventually, though, I knew the worst was over when Hook asked me for headache pills and a contribution to the police widows and orphans fund.

For actual news of the case we had to rely on Vanessa. Humberstones was, she said, her first port of call after leaving hospital. She looked radiant in a simple white blouse, with a black waistcoat and skirt. She kissed both Hubert and me and as she did so I suddenly remembered the letter tucked in my bag that Christopher had given me. She smiled as I handed it to her and slipped it unopened into her pocket.

'Thank you for your valiant effort, Kate. I really do appreciate it. My life has been transformed. I feel so . . . free.'

'I'm glad, Vanessa. You've had a rotten time.'

As I made coffee she said, 'I feel sorry for Sheila. She was so bitter and jealous. While we were alone she talked quite a bit. About the past, about the narrowness of her life, the loneliness. She began keeping tabs on me when she got the job at the farm. She worked there, you see, when Colin was in prison, just seasonal stuff, fruit pick-

ing, doing the accounts, selling eggs, that sort of thing.
That was where she first saw me, in Little Charnford.
From all she says the farmer had a soft spot for her. He
was over sixty and the farm was really too much for him
alone. When Colin came out of prison she could let him
stay in the caravan while she did jobs around the farm.
In deepest winter she was at the house in Bonsall, apart
from being at the farm one day a week. And of course she
had the use of the farm vehicles; the black van I saw—
that was her.'

'But why all the killing?' I asked.

Vanessa smiled bleakly. 'Panic, madness, wanting to
punish me, wanting me to be afraid. Wanting me to suffer as she'd suffered.'

'Why Colin?'

'Colin confessed, not so much in what he said but I
think she must have confronted him with . . . and he let it
be known she had made a terrible mistake.'

I sipped my coffee, still puzzled. 'Tell me, Vanessa.
Why didn't you tell me about Colin straight away?'

'I was desperate to put that time behind me. In some
way I felt that I was to blame, and all I wanted was to
forget the past. I couldn't even bear to say his name. But
then I realised the only way out was to be honest with
you.'

'Perhaps my visit to your sister caused her to go completely over the edge.'

'I think you're right, Kate.' Vanessa spoke calmly. 'So
Colin, too, had to die then for what he'd done. She
wanted us all to die, so that we could be together in a
better world.'

Vanessa sat silently then for some time. Hubert stared
out of the window. All that dying, all that misery, be-

cause one individual couldn't curb his lust for young girls.

'There's something else,' said Vanessa slowly, 'that I haven't come to terms with...' She paused as though having trouble telling me. 'And that is... Sheila isn't my sister, she's my mother.'

My mouth dropped open; Hubert turned in quick surprise from the window.

'I was born when Sheila was sixteen. My mother...no, not my mother, she was really my gran, was old when I was born but I never suspected. My real father disappeared as soon as Sheila knew she was pregnant. Somehow they managed to keep the birth a secret and I appeared as a menopausal baby. When Colin Tiffield came along she saw her chance to lead a normal life, get married, have another child that she really could call her own. I think for some of my life she really loved me but she was jealous. Jealous of the time and attention Mum, I mean Gran, gave me. When... Gran died that was my fault too.'

Hubert mumbled something then about 'tangled webs' and Vanessa managed to smile.

'Thank goodness Colin Tiffield didn't turn out to be my father. I think the burden of worrying about my having children with his genes in them would have been too much.'

I nodded in agreement.

As Vanessa turned to go she said, 'I'd like to keep in touch and I'm sorry I've caused you so much worry. If only I hadn't thought it was a man following me I might have noticed her. She used to walk around Longborough quite openly, you know. And I never noticed.'

'She was very clever,' I said. 'Near but not too near.'

'She was like that all my life,' said Vanessa sadly. 'It could have been different.'

Vanessa insisted that we need not show her out and we listened as her footsteps walked quickly and confidently down the stairs. From the window we watched as she approached her car. There was a figure in the car who stepped out to meet her. They talked for a moment and then walked off arm in arm along Longborough High Street.

'Well!' said Hubert. 'That's a turn up.'

'Good genes there,' I said. 'Well, respectable ones anyway.'

They looked a strange pair. Christopher with his arm in a sling, a baseball cap on his head and a spring in his step. A spring in both their steps. And Vanessa, as elegant from the back view as the front, walking unafraid, head held high.

'She's been lucky, unlike that poor girl dragged from the river.' Was she, too, the victim of some deadly admirer?

HARLEQUIN®

I N T R I G U E®

In steamy New Orleans, three women witnessed the same crime, testified against the same man and were then swept into the Witness Protection Program. But now, there's new evidence. These three women are about to come out of hiding—and find both danger and desire....

Start your new year right with all the books in the exciting EYEWITNESS miniseries:

#399 A CHRISTMAS KISS
by Caroline Burnes (December)

#402 A NEW YEAR'S CONVICTION
by Cassie Miles (January)

#406 A VALENTINE HOSTAGE
by Dawn Stewardson (February)

Don't miss these three books—or miss out on all the passion and drama of the crime of the century!

EYE1

CRIMINALS ALWAYS HAVE SOMETHING TO HIDE—BUT THE ENJOYMENT YOU'LL GET OUT OF A WORLDWIDE MYSTERY NOVEL IS NO SECRET....

With Worldwide Mystery on the case, we've taken the mystery out of finding something good to read every month.

Worldwide Mystery is guaranteed to have suspense buffs and chill seekers of all persuasions in eager pursuit of each new exciting title!

Worldwide Mystery novels—crimes worth investigating...

PAINTED TRUTH

LISE McCLENDON

First Time in Paperback

An Alix Thorssen Mystery

THE ART OF ILLUSION

Art expert/gallery owner Alix Thorssen is called on to appraise the charred remains of a friend's local gallery...a tragedy doubled when the body of artist Ray Thornton is found among the debris.

The death is ruled a suicide, the fire, arson. Case closed. But not for Alix, who believes the body in the fire was not Thornton's.

As her investigation forces her to confront her own foibles and contradictions as an art lover, another murder plot puts her in the hot seat as prime suspect. She must race to find a killer who knows that while life may imitate art...death makes it all the more profitable.

"Will leave you gasping..." —*Kirkus Reviews*

Available in December at your favorite retail stores.

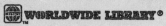

WORLDWIDE LIBRARY®

TRUTH

THE IRON GLOVE

First Time in Paperback

RONALD TIERNEY

A Deets Shanahan Mystery

THE NAKED LADY WASN'T YOUR AVERAGE FLOATER

She was, in fact, Sally Holland, wife of Indiana senator David Holland, half of Washington's Golden Couple. Within hours, a suspect is arrested—a young Latino boxer believed to be her lover. Though not at all convinced the police have the wrong suspect, private investigator Deets Shanahan nevertheless agrees to do some digging for the defense.

Another dead body later, along with some answers that just seem too easy and pat for a P.I. who has been around long enough to know the difference, Shanahan dives into the dirty side of politics and the dark side of passion—and the hideous secrets a killer is desperate to hide....

"A series packed with angles and delights."
—*Publishers Weekly*

Available in December at your favorite retail stores.

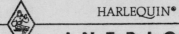

HARLEQUIN®

INTRIGUE®

THAT'S INTRIGUE—DYNAMIC ROMANCE AT ITS BEST!

Harlequin Intrigue is now bringing you more—more men and mystery, more desire and danger. If you've been looking for thrilling tales of contemporary passion and sensuous love stories with taut, edge-of-the-seat suspense—then you'll *love* Harlequin Intrigue!

Every month, you'll meet four new heroes who are guaranteed to make your spine tingle and your pulse pound. With them you'll enter into the exciting world of Harlequin Intrigue—where your life is on the line and so is your heart!

Harlequin Intrigue—we'll leave you breathless!

INT-GEN